PENGUIN BOOKS
LOVE OVER COFFEE

Amrit N. Shetty is an IT professional working with a multinational company. He has worked with various IT companies including ones in Austin, Dublin and Edinburgh. Besides writing, Amrit enjoys reading and watching movies. This is his debut novel.

He lives in Delhi with his wife. Read his blog at http://amritshetty.blogspot.com/

Love over Coffee

METRO
READS

Amrit N. Shetty

PENGUIN BOOKS

PENGUIN BOOKS

Published by the Penguin Group

Penguin Books India Pvt. Ltd, 11 Community Centre, Panchsheel Park,
New Delhi 110 017, India

Penguin Group (USA) Inc., 375 Hudson Street, New York,
New York 10014, USA

Penguin Group (Canada), 90 Eglinton Avenue East, Suite 700, Toronto,
Ontario, M4P 2Y3, Canada (a division of Pearson Penguin Canada Inc.)

Penguin Books Ltd, 80 Strand, London WC2R 0RL, England

Penguin Ireland, 25 St Stephen's Green, Dublin 2, Ireland
(a division of Penguin Books Ltd)

Penguin Group (Australia), 250 Camberwell Road, Camberwell,
Victoria 3124, Australia (a division of Pearson Australia Group Pty Ltd)

Penguin Group (NZ), 67 Apollo Drive, Rosedale, North Shore 0632,
New Zealand (a division of Pearson New Zealand Ltd)

Penguin Group (South Africa) (Pty) Ltd, 24 Sturdee Avenue, Rosebank,
Johannesburg 2196, South Africa

Penguin Books Ltd, Registered Offices: 80 Strand, London WC2R 0RL, England

First published by Penguin Books India 2010

Copyright © Amrit N. Shetty 2010

All rights reserved

10 9 8 7 6 5 4 3 2 1

ISBN 9780143066088

Typeset in Bembo Roman by SÜRYA, New Delhi
Printed at Manipal Press Ltd, Manipal

For

My mother and her dream for her son . . .

1

THE BEGINNING

It was a warm day. The sun was already high in the sky and even though summer was still a few weeks away, one could already feel the heat. We were driving down National Highway 8 in our metallic silver Santro. Dad was sitting next to me. It had been this way ever since I moved from Bangalore to live with my parents in Delhi.

Every morning I would drop Dad to work before driving another few miles to my office. In the evening I would pick him up on the way home. This arrangement not only saved Dad the effort of having to drive through the irrational Delhi traffic but it also gave me a valid excuse for not using the company transport. Taking the office bus meant that apart from having to abide by the strict timelines it also limited my movements during office hours. Having a car gave me and my friends the option to drive around when work at office was slack; an occasional run to the movies, shopping malls or for a drink, were always on the cards when our manager was out of office.

I was wearing my Ray-Ban sunglasses, a gift from Mom on my last birthday. I am usually bad at selecting things, but with these sunglasses it had been different. I had known which ones to pick the moment I had entered the store. It was probably Will Smith of *Men in Black*, who was instrumental in my selection. For the first few months I had worn them practically everyday while driving come rain or shine. The only time I drove without them was at night.

The fact that Rajni loved my glasses only helped their cause.

There were fewer cars on the road that day. Dad seemed happy. 'One of his contracts must have come through,' I thought. I was eager to start up a conversation, to kill time and to make the drive interesting.

'Dad, Neeraj got married last week. He married a colleague.'

'Neeraj! Is he not the guy you worked with in Bangalore?' Dad responded, still sounding happy.

'Yes Dad. His parents were initially against the marriage, but they finally relented,' I added.

'You kids in software—always travelling, falling in love and getting married with least regard to your parents' feelings. Taking the plunge when you would not have the maturity to understand what is best for you!' Dad retorted all of a sudden. I was taken aback. There was a slight annoyance in his voice.

I started concentrating on the road; the conversation was not such a good idea after all!

I began to think about Rajni instead. It was her birthday the next day and we were planning to organize a surprise party for her in the office. Well, to be honest, it was just me at the moment, but I was sure I could convince the others to join in too. There were so many things we needed to do, I thought with a sigh.

It also struck me that very soon I would have to tell Dad about Rajni. And if I had learnt anything from the conversation minutes ago, it was that Dad was not going to be so easy to convince. I braced myself for the future before shifting my concentration back on the road.

All of a sudden, the black Accent in front of us veered towards the left. To save us from an accident, I hit hard on the brakes, bringing our car to a screeching halt. A few seconds later, we were jolted by a loud jerk. The Maruti behind had rammed into us. What ensued was an argument between me and the owner of the car; it took a good one hour to resolve the issue and get back on the road to the office.

This was not how I had intended my day to start.

Meanwhile, Bhau had called in twice wanting to know the reason for my delay. Bhau, whose real name is Chetan Pardikar, had joined our company around the same time that I had. We got along like a house on fire right from day one. Chetan was from Maharashtra, where it is common to address a comrade as 'bhau'. What started as fun soon caught on and within a few months' time, no one bothered with his real name. He did not seem to mind either.

Chetan was a mentor for everyone around the office. He was like a tough coach who played things by the book. A stickler for perfection, efficiency and orderliness we found it hard to satisfy Bhau; he always ended up finding things to complain about. He had transformed himself into a parent-like figure, who would not bat an eyelid before chastising kids for their mistakes.

Every morning, Bhau waited for us to gather in the office, before heading for our daily tea in the cafeteria. Rajni, sometimes joined in, but usually it was just Bhau,

Parag, Subbu and me. Rajni loved the pohe that Bhau occasionally brought for breakfast. There would be a squabble between us to get a bigger share, but it was always Subbu who walked away with the most.

Rajni worked in a separate team which sat around the corner from where our desks were. I avoided meeting her inside the office, because she was paranoid about the rumour mills of our company. I would have continued trying to convince Rajni against her paranoia but for an incident. Rakshit, a member of Rajni's team, had gone out on a date with Anjali, another girl from the office, over the weekend. They were unlucky to have been spotted by some people from the office. On Monday the news about their rendezvous was all over the company like jungle fire—there was nothing more important than the talk about the two love birds.

I doubted if Bhau knew about my relationship with Rajni. I was sure he suspected there was something going on between us, but he never came out openly with his thoughts. Subbu and Parag, however, were in the know. Subbu knew because of his uncanny but unfortunate ability to appear at all the wrong places at the wrong times, and Parag, because I had told him.

I am not quite sure why I had disclosed our relationship only to Parag. It wasn't like I was closer to him than I was to Bhau and Subbu. We all were great friends and always hung out together. However, Parag was not only more mature but also more patient than any of us. He was like an undisturbed lake, calm and serene. Nothing seemed to trouble him and he managed to stay unruffled even in the toughest of situations. It was probably this maturity that had made me open up my thoughts to him.

Then again, Parag had been born under the sign of

Taurus, which was also Rajni's sun sign. This probably was the stronger of the reasons for my divulging my innermost secrets to him. I had never believed in sun signs before, but had picked up the habit of reading the horoscopes since I had met Rajni. Now I made it a point to regularly glance at the morning papers just to see what the day held for us before heading to office. Truth to tell, I read the five lines under Taurus first before reading the ones for Capricorn, my zodiac.

Sometimes I wondered how the same five lines could be true for both Rajni and Parag.

Only this morning I had read:

TAURUS (19 April–19 May): New friends are likely to enter your life. With the help of new friends, you may attain good career contacts, good fortune, new love energies and a variety of other goodies. Your stubbornness can sometimes cause friction on the home front. Find the right channel for your energy to avoid conflicts.

CAPRICORN (21 December–19 January): Don't be too ready to make changes to something that already works well. Your perspective will draw others to participate in your field. You may hurt someone with your behaviour. Be aware of how you affect others. Things may happen very fast and you will feel slightly out of control.

'Friction with family', I guessed, would hold true in Rajni's case all year long. Every date that I and Rajni had gone on started with the lament on how frustrated she was because of her fights with her mother or brother. I was led to believe that Rajni was the lone warrior against a horrid family which was bent on making her life miserable. I was determined to free my damsel from the clutches of her evil family, until our previous date at Nirula's, when I had spoken my thoughts aloud to Rajni.

And did I regret supporting her against the onslaught of her family!

I guess this should be a lesson to all the love-struck Romeos. I probably will never speak against her family again!

We left Nirula's that day, annoyed with each other. I decided that this was the end of our relationship. But, just as always, I was soon back on the phone trying to placate Rajni. It took me a week before we were back on talking terms.

There was a pattern emerging here which I was getting rather used to: we ended up fighting on dates and followed it up with a week of trying to make up to each other. So much so that we even took turns to fight and placate each other. It was these little fights that made our relationship interesting. Also, thinking about these fights now, bring a smile to my face.

The stubbornness that the horoscope mentioned did not surprise me. I was yet to meet someone who was as stubborn as Rajni. She was hard to shake once she believed in something. I had had my share of trouble due to her obstinacy. But what really caught my attention were the words '*With the help of new friends, you may attain good career contacts, good fortune, new love energies and a variety of other goodies.*'

I was going over these words in my head when the Maruti rammed into our car this morning.

~

'Bye, Dad!' I said as I pulled the car out of his office and drove on.

It was another twenty minutes before I reached my office, flashed my card in front of the card reader and waited for the barrier to slowly rise and make way for my car. I pulled the car into my regular parking slot No. 8 and walked towards the door that led to the main office area and climbed up one flight of stairs to the ground floor. The entrance door to the main building opened into the cafeteria. Though the lifts were available from the basement parking, I was in the habit of taking the stairs to the ground floor and then the lift from there.

As I walked across the cafeteria into the reception I saw Anjali, our office receptionist, at her desk concentrating on her computer screen, simultaneously talking on the phone. She had a frown on her face, it looked as if she was arguing with someone on the phone. My guess was that it was Rakshit. She was wearing a bright red salwar kameez and lipstick to match. Had I known her well, I would probably have told her about how I hated bright lipsticks.

Fortunately, Rajni never wore too much make-up. In fact, the only time I remember her wearing make up was when we had gone to attend a common friend's wedding. Rajni had worn a dark brown saree and a rather dark shade of lipstick to go with it. She looked beautiful that night. All the attention she'd got from the people around, including a pesky photographer, had made me jealous. I had wished that I could have collected all the photographs he had taken that day and stored them safely where no one other than me would have been able to see them.

Anjali and Rakshit were getting married next month.

The marriage probably was a culmination of the rumours at our company. I wondered how things would have turned out if Rajni and I had been spotted instead. We always avoided crowded areas and limited ourselves to either Nirula's or the basement parking. We only went to shopping malls or restaurants when we were accompanied by a group of friends.

'Good morning, Anjali,' I said as I passed her on my way towards the lifts.

She looked up from the computer screen and gave a questioning smile that seemed to say, 'Is this the time to get to the office?'

I smiled back at her as I entered the lift.

I pressed the button for the fourth floor and turned towards the mirrored rear wall of the lift to check my hair. I was wearing a blue shirt and navy trousers.

As I walked out of the lift, desperate to see Rajni, I was tempted to glance around the corner to see if I could spot her. But I spotted Subbu instead. He was at the coffee machine.

'Hi, Subbu. Good morning!' I said cheerfully cursing him under my breath. He sure had a way of appearing in all the wrong places!

'Want some coffee?' he asked. Then not bothering to wait for my answer, he filled a second cup and headed towards me. I took my coffee from his hand, and we walked towards our seating area.

Subbu had the habit of taking decisions for others. He assumed that people would always want what he wants. It annoyed me at times but mostly I ignored it knowing fully well that he was only trying to help.

Subbu had also moved in from Chennai around the

same time that I had joined the company. Subbu, Bhau, Parag and I had attended the induction trainings together.

The induction trainings are a part of the organizational initiative to help a new employee get acclimatized to the organization. The length of these trainings and the topics covered depended on whether one was a fresher or an experienced hand. At our company, the trainings for freshers lasted about three months and included rigorous training on the software platform to be slotted to the person. On the other hand the experienced lot, having already worked on the relevant software platforms, did not have to go through such extensive training.

The best part about these induction trainings was that they were conducted at external locations, usually star hotels. They were like paid holidays, where you did not have much to do other than listening to boring lectures. If you were smart, you could catch a wink or two before lunch or tea was served!

The lunch was always good because the human resource team overdid themselves, trying to impress the new employees. The truth about the company was always hidden till the employee made it to one of the project teams.

We had learnt about Subbu's love for sweets during our induction, when we had spotted him hovering around the sweets counter. Apart from sweets Subbu also loved eating curd rice and idlis.

I had a soft corner for idlis too.

For the first few days during the induction training Subbu's Hindi had been a butt of jokes with us but we soon stopped trying to correct him or to make fun. He wasn't shy of trying to speak in a new language. Subbu also had the same approach to eating. He was never to be dissuaded from trying out new food or delicacies. It had cost him a bad stomach or two but that didn't change anything.

As we walked by, KK looked up from his seat. He seemed really annoyed.

KK, or Kiran Kumar, was our manager and he was rather touchy about everything.

It annoyed KK if you were late to office. KK got angry if you left early or were missing from your desk for a long time. KK became anxious when you missed your project deadlines. He was hyper when you failed to deliver even after being reminded about the impending deadline more than once. KK hated it when people were late for meetings. He was all over you if you made mistakes in your deliverables. In other words, a regular boss.

I had faced KK's music when I had missed an entire set of modules because of an oversight. I still don't understand why KK had made such a fuss; it wasn't like I had killed someone!

I sometimes thought that Bhau would someday grow into KK's shoes. There was so much Bhau and KK had in common; being sticklers for efficiency was one such thing.

KK even kept a note of all such failings of his team. These notes were used to rate the employee during the annual appraisal.

I was sure he recorded my late coming. He would bring it up in our mid-year session if not during the evening's team meeting. He wasn't a bad person, but he did sometimes get on your nerves because of his quest for perfection and insistence on playing everything by the rules.

He was always either busy with PowerPoint presentations and Microsoft Project charts or in making Excel spreadsheets. Kiran had a spreadsheet for everything. Without a doubt he maintained one tracking the time we got to office.

'Good morning, Kiran,' I greeted him as I walked to my cubicle.

Kiran nodded before getting back to whatever he was doing. If I had to make a guess, he was probably working on what other spreadsheets he could conjure up in order to make our lives more difficult!

There was another facet to time-keeping that got to you if you sat and wondered about it. Our company had initially installed card readers at the door to check and record the 'in' and 'out' times of the employee. The process was soon done away with. The management sent around a mail stating that the card readers were only instrumental for the security of the employees and not for recording the time. The management added that since all the employees were smart and capable of watching over themselves, the additional checks were no longer necessary. Few months later, there was another mail asking the managers to keep a track of their employees' 'in' and 'out' timings.

All this would have confused anyone new to an IT company, but for us employees, these were a part of normal functioning.

So, in all, we ended up with the card readers that I am sure still sends reports of employee 'in' and 'out' times to managers, coupled with the additional checks that managers maintain on their own!

Maybe it was wrong to blame KK alone for our

predicament with his spreadsheets. He probably was a victim of the process like us. However, KK in his zeal to remain ahead of the management demands overdid everything.

I placed my coffee on the desk and looked out through the glass window behind my chair.

Subbu was sitting in his cubicle across mine. There was an aisle that separated our cubicles. Each floor in the office, except for the ground floor reception area, was more or less similar in design. At one end of each floor, there were the elevators with two coffee machines near them; the cubicles took up the length of the room and meeting rooms were placed at the other end.

Each floor had two meeting rooms and a large conference hall. On our floor the conference hall had been converted into a library. The meeting rooms on each floor had names. On our floor they were called 'Sydney' and 'Austin' after the two places where our company had branches. When we had moved into the building the HR team had sent mails asking for suggestions to name the meeting rooms. Bhau, Subbu, Parag and I had not bothered with them but from what we heard there were more than a hundred responses!

A week after the competition was formally closed the HR team disclosed the names with much fanfare. What bothered me most was the lack of creativity among my colleagues. I concluded that the selection of names had more to do with pleasing the higher management.

My team was located at the cubicles to the right side facing the coffee machine while Rajni's team sat around the corner on the left hand side. This setup was a hindrance for me, because I could not see Rajni from my desk. I had to walk down to the coffee machine in order to steal a glance at her from time to time.

Subbu and Parag loved to pull my leg when I did that. KK also must have felt that there was something funny about me and the coffee machine. I dreaded that he would corner me one day and ask for an explanation for the giggling that happened each time I headed for coffee; and he probably had an Excel spreadsheet recording the number of times, too!

The restrooms were located on the same end as the meeting rooms. We either had to walk all the way around the floor, along the wall, from where we sat or walk the aisle between the lift and the coffee machine and then take a right to get to the restrooms.

There was little doubt as to which route I preferred.

2

OF POTATOES AND ONIONS

'Let's go for lunch,' Bhau suggested, raising his head from the cubicle.

It was nearly noon.

The cafeteria began serving lunch at 12.00.

I was onto my fourth cup of coffee, which, considering the fact that I had arrived in office at about ten, was a little on the higher side.

I was getting a little desperate. I had been unable to spot Rajni since the time I got in. She had not been there at her desk when I had gone to collect the coffees.

I had already sent her fifteen emails. The first email had been my regular morning one with the subject: 'Good morning!'

I had followed that up a little later with subjects like: 'Where are you?'

'Angry?'

'Sorry!'

'Hey, don't do this on the eve of your birthday!'

'I am not having lunch today.'

And finally, 'WHAT @?'

There was still no reply from her. I'd sent the last few messages with a request for a return receipt, but none of them had been opened.

Subbu was beginning to clean up his desk which was an indication that he was ready to leave for lunch.

If there was anything Subbu loved more than food, it had to be his fetish for keeping his desk squeaky clean. Subbu was the kind of guy who spent a lot of time every day ensuring that all the unnecessary bits and pieces of paper left lying around on his desk ended in the shredder.

Subbu's love and passion for cleanliness would get under anyone's skin. Imagine having to sit next to him!

I still remember the time when Subbu had taken his love of orderliness to a new high, or rather a poorly low, by shredding KK's spreadsheets. It had happened the day KK had come by to my desk needing a few updates on a project. He had unknowingly placed his documents, which included spreadsheet printouts about everything and anything, on Subbu's desk.

'So Anup, why did you charge less time for the project last week?' asked KK.

'I don't think I . . .' I responded, more out of habit than anything else.

At the back of my mind was the realization that KK must have it all recorded on his spreadsheets. There was no way I was going to be able to talk my way out of this. I had a premonition of what was coming.

'I checked the status report for the week, and you don't seem to have completed the components. Do you realize that our target for delivery is by the month's end? I doubt you have even started work on them,' KK continued severely.

'But . . . but . . .' I stammered not knowing what to do. I caught Parag and Subbu out of the corner of my eye. They were enjoying this.

Bhau, however, was busy working at his terminal.

How a person could continue working while KK was harassing me in the next cubicle, I couldn't understand. Watching Bhau work unconcerned had increased my frustration. If only Bhau had not been so prompt with his deliverables!

Subbu, who was behind KK, had started making faces at me. I found it hard to control my laughter.

My reaction annoyed KK even more.

'Stop giggling! Let me show you the figures,' KK shouted before turning around to retrieve his spreadsheets from Subbu's desk.

KK was in for a surprise! The spreadsheets and all the paperwork that he had brought with him were missing.

Here's what had happened: Subbu, who had returned from a cigarette break, a few minutes ago, had noticed that his desk was not as clutter free as he had left it. He saw a whole lot of meaningless printouts on the desk.

Needless to say what fate the humongous, meticulously prepared paperwork had met then.

To a large extent, I was to be blamed for KK's predicament. I had nothing personal against cleanliness, but I hated Subbu's finickiness about it. In defiance I had made it a point to place any document that needed to go into the trash or shredder on Subbu's desk. The first time I did that Subbu had got annoyed, but he soon caught on to my trick and no sooner would he discover any document that did not belong to him he would send it down the shredder. We had become so engrossed in our daily game that Subbu never bothered to check what the documents were or who they belonged to.

The fact that Subbu was not at his desk when KK appeared didn't help.

Now Subbu was also one of those people who, if they felt were being unjustly treated or victimized, could go to any lengths fighting for their rights. Even KK was aware of that. He knew the solution: never to confront Subbu unless you really had to.

So when KK shouted out, 'Where are my documents!' Parag and I burst out laughing. Bhau stood up, leaving his computer for once, to see what was happening. KK stood there fuming—red as a ripe tomato. And Subbu?

Subbu, just gaped like a monkey, trying to understand what went wrong, before blurting out, 'I am sorry, sir . . .'

We haven't yet forgotten the look on his face at that moment.

KK had been so annoyed that he had walked away without bothering to wait for an explanation.

I breathed a sigh of relief.

That day Bhau, Parag, Subbu and I were in the office until the wee hours, completing all my pending components.

Subbu had been annoyed with me, 'If you had done some coding instead of spending all the time on Rajni . . .' By the time we left, all the restaurants around office had closed and he had had to go without dinner that night.

It felt great to have such caring friends. I bore the brunt of all their grumbling without a complaint.

I was a lucky good-for-nothing ass!

~

'Lunch,' said Subbu, standing up after having cleaned up the last trespassing nano-particle from his desk. Then he walked into my cubicle and stood behind me staring at my computer screen, his eyes boring through my head, trying to read every word on my screen. It annoyed me when Subbu sneaked behind me like this, catching me unprepared.

'Subbu, can't you see that I am doing something personal?' I said, but it had hardly made a difference. He had not only unabashedly read my mails but even felt qualified enough to pass judgement. 'Anup, all you ever do is type sorry mails to Rajni. Is there a single day that goes by without a fight between the two of you?'

I would have punched his face that day if I could. Just the fact that Subbu was very strong and well built prevented me from doing so. He was attractive in his own way for the girls though. They always flocked around his desk.

It always annoyed Rajni when she spotted the girls near my desk. It did not matter that they were probably visiting Subbu.

Rajni looked beautiful when she was angry. Rajni always looked beautiful, but, when angry, she looked even better. Her annoyance at the girls filled me with joy. I loved it when the proverbial green-eyed monster struck her.

I locked my computer and was about to stand up when I heard a group of people approaching us.

～

We spotted Priyanka walking towards KK's desk with a group of new employees in tow. She was wearing a black shirt and cream-coloured trousers, and looked like a beauty queen walking the ramp. I am sure none the new employees complained about having to walk around the office behind her. I am also sure that the new employees hardly remembered anything about the people Priyanka introduced them to.

It was a good policy on the company's part to let Priyanka run the introductions. The new employees were so smitten for the first few weeks following the introductions that they could not stop raving about how good the organization was.

I am sure HR did have other reasons for recruiting beautiful girls.

Our company's Human Resources team was full of them.

I had once made the mistake of mentioning this to Rajni who had argued vehemently about how wrong I was. She then stopped speaking to me for a week following the incident!

~

Priyanka was a tall, dusky, ravishing beauty and Parag thought she would give Bipasha a run for her money if she were to set foot in Bollywood! She had long, jet black hair that she always let hang free and from time to time she used her hand to brush the hair away from her face, an action which transfixed all the men.

I felt a little guilty standing there and adoring the beautiful Priyanka. I wondered what Rajni would think if she read my thoughts.

Then again, I was annoyed with her for not having replied to any of my mails, it served her right!

I looked at Subbu. He was standing still; he did not blink his eyes even once. I personally did not have a problem with that, but for the fact that it was hard to stand up while Subbu continued standing like a pillar behind me.

Priyanka and the new employees walked up to KK. They stood there watching the beautiful Priyanka run the introductions, followed by some questions directed at the manager for their benefit. They also got an opportunity to resolve their queries. We noticed KK was smiling from ear to ear while replying to the questions. I had never seen him so cheerful. Given half a chance he would have loved to run Priyanka through all his innumerable spreadsheets, I was sure.

Bhau had learnt from KK that one of the new employees would be joining our team. KK always confided in Bhau. This was in a way good for us, because Bhau shared all the big and not so big changes in the organization and team with us, before they were revealed by KK in the team meetings.

KK loved to surprise us with his updates during team meetings. He took great delight in watching how uneasy we got when he announced these changes. He was like the fisherman who loves to watch the fish squirm and fight when they are pulled out of water, entangled in the net. The more helpless we looked, the happier he got!

I had come to dread KK's team meetings.

Priyanka turned suddenly, having finished her discussion with KK, catching me and Subbu unprepared. I fell back into my chair, disturbing Bhau from his stupor. He looked up momentarily, before going back to his green and black screen.

Priyanka had noticed us and was well aware of the effect she had on men, sometimes using this knowledge to her advantage. Subbu, however did not stop staring at Priyanka. It made me uneasy but Priyanka smiled and waved at him before heading off with her flock of slaves to the next manager.

Subbu stirred for the first time since Priyanka had made her appearance.

'Lunch?' piped Parag, smiling at me.

I checked my emails, hoping that Rajni had replied, before walking along with the rest to the cafeteria.

There was still no mail from Rajni.

~

I walked ahead, leading the way, lest Bhau had other ideas about taking the shorter route.

I reached the lift and stood there waiting for the others, knowing well that Bhau would insist on taking the steps.

My plan did not escape Subbu who whispered into my ear, 'Oh, she is still not at her desk, we could have taken the shorter route.'

I continued walking, ignoring Subbu's comment. Rajni was not at her desk. My heart sunk, not spotting her since morning. I wondered if she felt the same about me. As we walked past the coffee machine, I noticed Payal.

Payal was Rajni's best friend in the office. They were inseparable. For a moment I considered walking to Payal's seat to ask her about Rajni's whereabouts, but dropped the idea soon enough. It was so hard to understand Rajni. She had not even told her best friend about our relationship!

Rajni did not trust anyone.

Rajni also got furious at anything I did to jeopardize our secret.

Over the months I had built a list of things that I wasn't supposed to do, according to Rajni. Had I maintained a spreadsheet, I probably would have put KK to shame.

1) I was not permitted to talk to Rajni's friends about the relationship.
2) I was allowed only one call per day to Rajni's desk phone.
3) A few extra calls were allowed on special occasions but even then the number could not exceed four.
4) I was not to discuss anything I and Rajni did on dates with my friends.
5) I should never be seen alone with Rajni by any of our colleagues at work.
6) I was not allowed to call her home phone unless Rajni gave me a missed call first.
7) It was a given that Rajni would never call my number because of the risk involved if one of her family members spotted my number on the telephone bills.

The list became longer with time.

I sometimes wondered how I still managed to continue loving Rajni; but I did.

I loved Rajni and abided by all her rules.

~

I walked on without giving Payal a second thought. I was sure Subbu saw right through me, he was a mind reader and my face was an open book to him. It did make me very uneasy around him, but thankfully Subbu was always on my side. I knew inside the hard exterior that he projected, there was a soft man.

I had learnt from one of Subbu's old friends that he had moved to Delhi in order to stay away from memories that haunted him in Chennai. It was something to do with a girl he fell in love with. Subbu never spoke of the past. He had once chastened me into silence when I had broached the subject. He seldom displayed his pains and usually came across as a fun loving man who had no complaints against life. In all the time I had spent with Subbu I had seen him sad only once, on the day the girl he loved was getting married. Even then Subbu had not disclosed the reason. He just sat in one corner with a drink in hand, tears knocking at his eyes.

There was a marriage invitation card lying in front of him with letters printed in Tamil.

I controlled my desire to console Subbu and walked out with the drink, leaving him alone with his past. As I stood on the balcony staring into the emptiness, I shuddered as I recollected the words from a Jagjit Singh song, 'Why is the end of every meeting a separation . . .'

I wondered how I would have taken it had Rajni and I been separated instead of Subbu and Syalini, and I felt tears trickle down my eyes. Unlike Subbu, I could not stop them from flowing freely.

I cried in remorse for the emptiness that Subbu felt inside him.

I cried in remorse for the pain that I feared would befall me.

I cried because I wanted to run away from everything that my life had given me till then.

~

The smell from the cafeteria wafted towards us as we pushed open the door leading to it. It was beginning to fill up with people. The cafeteria had a small snacks counter at its centre which served soft drinks, juices, pastries, samosas, sandwiches and other ready-to-eat snacks. We usually walked down to the cafeteria for a quick bite every evening before heading home.

We picked our trays and joined what we thought was the shortest queue. Subbu had found us a table by the time I finished helping myself to the food. We sat eating quietly, no one wanting to break the silence.

I was thinking about where Rajni had disappeared; Bhau was probably immersed in thoughts of the program he was writing; Parag was his blissful self; and Subbu was eating, in between taking stock of the new girls he spotted in the cafeteria.

'Hi, can I join you guys?' said a voice, breaking us away from our thoughts.

It was AM.

What did he want from us?

It was not every day that AM took time to speak to the potatoes and onions of software industry because he was rather busy making space for himself at the top.

AM or Arun Mehra was hated by everyone at our level in the organization.

He had swiftly climbed the organizational ladder, leaving people like us where we rightly belonged—at the bottom. He was as adored by the higher management as he was hated by lower levels. He left a trail of onions and potatoes that he loved cutting through wherever he went.

AM had his views on the software industry which he once made a mistake of sharing at a team party.

'A software engineer is nothing but a common potato or an onion. You can cut them, cook them and eat them. Once their work is done, you can just go to the market and buy a whole lot more! It is the higher management, the managers that are valuable,' he had said.

We had been too drunk to care.

Parag had a wise smirk on his face; he probably was imagining himself on the vegetable shelf.

Then AM had gone on to win the 'Employee of the Quarter' the next month, followed by the 'Employee of the Year' award that year. Soon he got promoted as team leader. The last I had heard was that AM had travelled to New Jersey for a major project.

No matter how inane it sounds, it is true that an IT professional who has not yet made it to the rungs of higher management is just a potato or an onion.

Actually, an IT professional is either a potato or an onion.

The potatoes are easy to cook and readily mix with other vegetables. There is no limit as to what one can do with a potato. The onions on the other hand are harder to manage. They have a strong flavour of their own and when cut can make one cry. A good IT team is one where there is a proper mix of onions and potatoes. More the number of onions the harder it is to manage the team, as onions always revolt and want to rise quickly. Higher number of potatoes, on the other hand, drastically bring down the quality of deliverables. The fact that these vegetables tend to transmogrify from one to another, time to time, makes the task of managing the team very challenging. There is constant correction required.

It is also very important to remember that these vegetables have a shelf life. A potato when spoilt just dies its own death while the onion starts stinking.

~

Subbu stood up.

'Want something from the counter?' he asked no one in particular walking down for a second helping.

'I want some onions,' replied Parag. I smiled, catching on.

Bhau gave us his usual no-nonsense stare.

We suppressed our smiles and continued eating.

'Can you please get me a gulab jamun too?' requested AM.

AM was not just sitting at our table, he was also trying to involve us in a meaningful conversation! I sensed something fishy. Requesting a favour from his junior was out of line with his conduct, I thought; ordering would have more befitted his style!

Whatever happened to his belief in the Dilbert principle that stated 'Never eat lunch with a person of lower salary.'

Subbu returned with the sweets and some cut onions.

We finished our lunch quickly and asked AM to excuse us before beating a hasty retreat.

3

THE COFFEE MACHINE

'What do you think AM wanted from us?' asked Subbu as we walked past the new buildings that were spurting around our office.

Subbu, Parag, Bhau and I were in the habit of going for a short walk every afternoon after lunch. The walk also provided Subbu and Parag a chance to smoke.

'Give me a puff,' I said, taking the cigarette from Parag.

Though I did not smoke on a regular basis I needed this cigarette to collect my thoughts about Rajni. The lunch with AM was another reason.

'Let's go back. I have to finish coding the module and run a few tests,' said Bhau.

When we walked back to office still wondering what AM had wanted from us, we found KK sitting at his desk. He looked busy with one of his spreadsheets. He did not seem his usual self.

Whatever it was, he was sure to announce it at the team meeting that evening.

The team meeting was scheduled for 4.00 p.m. every Thursday, which, KK said, had something to do with the reports he had to send off on Fridays. The team meeting helped KK take stock of the progress made during the week and also to plan on how to torment us the following week.

I walked back to my seat and logged on to my computer.

The first thing I did was to check my mails. There was one mail from Rajni.

My heart skipped a beat.

'What is wrong with you?' the subject of the email read.

What is wrong with me?

'I was worried about you. Where the hell have you been? You know that I have to see you first thing in the morning!' I replied.

'None of your business, you have filled my mailbox. Payal was at my desk when I logged on. She must have seen all your emails. How many times have I told you not to write anything on the subject of the mail? I am really angry. Please do not email me for the next hour and don't even try calling me on my desk phone,' was Rajni's reply.

I stared at the email. I reread it a number of times for the next ten minutes.

I cursed Payal and wondered how I was going to get through the next hour.

I knew better than to try calling Rajni or emailing her, so I flipped over to the green and black screen hoping to catch up on all the pending work. I opened KK's assignment spread sheet and found my name against the module 'JPMF34HK'. I opened the component design for the module from the respective project folder and started reading.

Add code to check the 'Affinity' table for changes and initiate the relevant JPMF**HK module depending on the changed row.

On a successful return from the called module, generate a report for all the updates.

Use defined standards for all the changes.

I wondered what the 'Affinity' table was. It was funny how people wrote component designs that were so hard to decipher. I sat there imagining myself at a military base trying to crack the code for the latest message intercepted from enemy lines. Then spent another fifteen minutes trying to make head or tail of the module name.

Finally, I gave up and walked to Bhau's desk. 'Bhau, can you please look at the component design for "JPMF34HK"?' I requested.

Bhau looked up at me, annoyed. He pouted his lips before blowing out a fresh gust of air from his mouth. I could tell that he was frustrated at my troubling him. He probably was in the middle of breaking a code. He sometimes acted like he was working on something as important as designing a satellite or a rocket missile.

If it had been someone who did not know Bhau or what Bhau did, he would have mistaken Bhau for a scientist in a research lab in line for the next Nobel Prize! Such was his dedication . . . He had a thin frame and a face that gleamed with determination and steadfastness, which sometimes frightened people away. The lines on his firm cheeks and forehead made him look older than his age.

I subdued my emotions and requested again, 'Please Bhau, the component design is not making sense to me.'

We spent the next twenty minutes breaking the code.

Bhau finally said, 'That is a simple change,' before letting me walk back to my seat, perplexed as ever.

I knew Bhau was different from the beginning, when we had met him at the induction training. He was not someone you could fall in love with in the first meeting. He needed time to settle into your heart. He needed time to make you a part of his life. In a perfect world people like Bhau would be the most coveted assets but sadly the world is far from perfect. I knew it was always a wrong idea to approach him for help when he was busy working on his code. It was as if he had been transported to a different world altogether. I had known of times when Bhau spent nights in office, helping others complete their code. He found joy in watching the lines of code work. It was something that gave him the utmost satisfaction.

While we only wrote lines of code that managed to hold together and at times even work, Bhau breathed life into them. He was an artist when it came to coding with COBOL. Sadly there is no place in IT for such artists.

Meanwhile nothing stopped people, like me, from using him to meet their ends. And him from working relentlessly, unaware that in life people are judged not so much by things that they have done but more often by things they have not.

~

I looked at the clock—ten more minutes to go before I could email Rajni.

I switched back to KK's spreadsheet hoping to find something simpler and less cryptic than 'JPMF34HK'.

I did not fare any better trying to understand 'JPMF44HK', 'JPMF36HK' and 'JPMF74HK' which were the other modules that had been assigned against my name.

I opened my mailbox and started typing a new email to Rajni.

'I am sorry. What do you want for your birthday tomorrow?'

I reread the email before pressing the send button, happy that I had scanned it a few times for things that might tell Payal something if she inadvertently spotted it.

'I don't want anything. I am on leave tomorrow. Don't try to call me tomorrow. I am going out with Mom to the temple, and then we will all be going out for dinner,' was Rajni's reply.

She seemed angry.

'But, I thought we could go out for lunch! Are you not giving us a party?' I replied.

How could she do this to me? It was her birthday. *I* wanted to spend time with her.

Rajni was sometimes difficult to understand. I had always felt that she was the most important part of my life. I was even ready to sacrifice everything I had, if it could guarantee that Rajni would be mine; I had dreamt so many dreams for the two of us. I even had so many things going on in my mind about how to celebrate her birthday. But she could only think of her family's happiness.

I swallowed my pride and pain.

There was nothing I could have done because I was in love with Rajni.

When I look back at those days, I think Rajni had done what she had, not because she loved me less, but because she loved me in a way that I never could love her. She was not trying to win me over but instead was just happy to be a part of me. While I struggled to take control of

Rajni's life—struggled for ways to display my love and assure myself that she was mine—Rajni always knew that we were one. It was a dilemma that I could never have understood then, but it did make things harder for us. I wish I could go back to those days and let Rajni know that I understand. I never did come to know Rajni's bit of the story, but I somehow never felt the need to ask her.

'We can go out on Monday. I have to throw a party for the others, too,' read Rajni's next email.

'We', 'others'—what exactly did Rajni have in mind? There was no point arguing with her.

'Can we meet now for a few minutes? I have to talk to you.' I asked, desperate to see her, to talk to her. I wanted to be close to Rajni and feel her warmth next to me. I wanted to smell her sweet perfume. I wanted to watch that gleam in her eyes as she told me about all that had happened since we had last met. I wanted to assure myself that Rajni was still mine. And if Rajini was not coming in to work tomorrow, it was even more important that we met today.

'No! Not today. I have a lot to do.'

'Please, Rajni, you aren't even coming in tomorrow. I need to see you!' I hoped she would understand how desperate I was to meet her.

'Okay, but only for fifteen minutes. Come down to your car at 3.45. Don't be late, and stop emailing me. I have work to do!'

I sighed with relief, but the question still bothered me—why could we not meet in the cafeteria or in the library like all the other people did? Why did we always have to meet surreptitiously?

And suddenly, I was struck by the similarity between

the cryptic component designs and Rajni, both equally enigmatic.

~

I was up from my seat at precisely 3.30.

I looked around at others: Subbu was busy on the phone convincing someone that he had indeed paid the bill on time. I guess he was arguing with the mobile phone company.

Bhau seemed immersed in coding, blissfully unaware of the world around him.

Parag was probably still dreaming about how he could make his life a little more fun or advising someone on the same topic. All I could see was the top of his head from where I stood.

I walked out, hoping that Subbu and Parag would remain busy with what they were doing and not notice me. Bhau was still too deep into his research to be worried about my whereabouts.

I had just turned left for the lift and was about to pass KK's cubicle.

'Anup, how is the work progressing?' I heard KK enquire.

'Darn!' I cursed my luck and KK before adding, 'Work is progressing well. I am working on the modules from the spread sheet.'

'Very good!' KK replied. Then he paused a little before adding: 'Anup, I want a list of all the modules that can be tested independently. Could you please get me one before the meeting?'

I was getting late for my meeting with Rajni. She would be waiting for me at the car. It was virtually impossible for me come up with the list before the meeting, even if I had had nothing else to do! It was certainly not my day today!

I racked my brains for a solution.

Rajni had not been in a good mood since morning and getting late was not going to help in appeasing her. If I cancelled the meeting now, she would be furious. Also, I could not ask anyone to inform Rajni that I was not going to be able to meet her as that would mean confiding about our arrangement to meet and more so about the relationship. Though Parag and Subbu knew all about me and Rajni, and I was sure Rajni knew that they did, she still wanted to keep everything hidden and a secret. I also did not want Rajni waiting alone near the car. It was lonely in the parking lot. But more than anything else I wanted to see Rajni.

The only way that I could still manage to make it to the basement car park in time was by convincing Subbu to complete the task for me. I hurried back to Subbu's seat and unsuccessfully tried requesting, pleading and begging him, before finally agreeing to buying him a drink at Shiva's. That did the trick! Subbu agreed to prepare the list for me.

I checked the time in my watch. It was already 3.45!

I hurried to the lift not bothering about someone noticing me. When the lift finally came up, I jumped in and pressed '−1' hoping that no one from the floors below wanted to use the lift and praying at the same time that Rajni was still waiting.

With my heart pounding away in my chest, I restlessly watched the numbers change on the display.

I was worried about the list KK had wanted me to get ready before the meeting.

I was worried about what KK would have in store for me at the meeting.

I was worried whether Subbu would complete the list before the meeting.

I was worried about what was going on in Rajni's mind at the moment.

I was afraid that Rajni would have returned after having waited for me at the car park. I wondered what I would do if I did find Rajni near the car.

My heart beat faster as I neared the basement.

It was forty seconds past 3.46 when I finally hit the bottom.

I ran towards my car.

Thankfully, Rajni was still there.

I stood still, watching Rajni, while trying to catch my breath.

She was looking radiant in an orange shirt and black trousers, leaning against the window, peering inside my car trying to take stock of the things inside.

'I am sorry I'm late,' I managed between gasps.

Rajni looked up, turning towards me. She looked beautiful with her curly hair falling loosely on her shoulders.

I loved the way Rajni's hair danced when she shook her head. She was very fair and a little on the heavier side—not fat but just plump enough to look the way she did, cute. I loved watching her laugh—her head rolled back and her cheeks dimpled.

I wished I could have continued looking at her for ever. I remember having once told her how I felt about her. It had made her blush. The memory has stayed with me.

I was sure Rajni knew of the effect the shirt had on me. I wanted to hold Rajni tight and never let her go . . . I wanted to make Rajni mine forever. I stood there transfixed by my beautiful damsel, forgetting everything about KK, component designs, team meetings and AM and would have stayed that way forever. There was nothing else I wanted from life.

'You are late! I have been waiting here worrying that somebody might come down. You are so very callous Anup,' she said angrily.

'I am really sorry, dear, but KK caught me just when I was about to leave,' I managed before adding, 'Thank you for meeting me, you look beautiful!'

That quelled Rajni's anger a little. She was beginning to blush. I could see her beautiful little nose turning pink. It was hard to stop myself from reaching out to her. And touching her. I wanted to feel her hands in mine. I wanted to kiss her cheeks, smell her sweet perfume.

I wanted to assure myself that Rajni was all mine.

'Okay, tell me, what do you want? You have sent me so many emails since morning. Can't you understand that I would have replied had I been at my desk? Payal was sitting by my side when I logged on. She must have seen all your emails, with the silly subject lines that you write.' Rajni said still trying to sound angry but I could sense that she was cooling down.

'Why are you not coming in tomorrow? I wanted to be the first person to wish you on your birthday. I thought we could go out for lunch and then I could buy you a gift,' I said nearly pleading.

'Kyaaaaaaaaa hain, please don't do this naaaaaaaaa Anup,' said Rajni putting up a false frown.

I loved the way Rajni said that. Rajni stressed on the 'a' like she was singing the sentence out.

'I had promised Mama that I would take a holiday on my birthday. We can go out on Monday. And, please do not get me any gifts. It is hard explaining to my parents about the expensive stuff that you bring,' said Rajni as she blew her hair away from her face.

Rajni's hair was like her, very stubborn. It seemed to have a mind of its own—always kept slipping back to her face. There was nothing more beautiful than watching Rajni blow her hair away from her face.

'But, Rajni, it is your birthday,' I managed before blurting out, 'I love you!'

I noticed her cheeks turning a deep pink.

'On Monday you will have all your friends in tow. I wanted to go somewhere alone with you,' I added making up a sad face.

'No, not next week, we can go sometime later. I am very busy next week. I need to take Payal, Nidhi and Ashish out too. They will kill me if I don't give them a treat,' Rajni smiled as she said that.

I could sense that her anger had completely disappeared.

We stood there in the basement, next to my car, talking for the next ten minutes about everything Rajni had done that day. She had been asked by her manager to create a training plan for the new joinees. It surely was good news because the assignment of training new people was something the managers reserved for the best people they had. She seemed very excited about the new responsibility. Besides she was very hard working. She had always been in the good books of all the managers she had worked with. It helped that Rajni looked beautiful. But I was sure even if Rajni had not been so beautiful she would have done just as well.

I know many people who would disagree with me about the last bit, one of them being Subbu.

Subbu always felt that beautiful girls in IT had an advantage over others. He felt that the male mangers always fell for their charm and ended up being partial to them.

~

I looked at my watch. It was 4.05.

'Oh, shit!' I blurted, 'I had a meeting at four o'clock. I need to rush back!' Then I stopped for a second, 'Bye, and happy birthday,' I said pulling myself away from Rajni. 'I love you a lot!'

I rushed back to the lift.

I was annoyed at having to leave Rajni so soon. Deciding to call her up the next day I entered the lift. And the euphoria soon made way for anxiety.

I reached our floor and rushed to my seat.

The seats were all empty. Everyone had left for the meeting.

I quickly collected my notebook before rushing to Austin.

The idea of walking into Austin would have sounded funny at other times, but right now I was in no mood for fun.

'Austin' or 'Sydney'—I failed to see the fun.

'Excuse me, please,' I said as I opened the door.

KK was busy describing something.

I had cut him short.

He turned his face and looked straight at me—angry because of the interruption.

I completely forgot about my meeting with Rajni as I waited at the door for KK's reaction.

I knew he was always looking for an opportunity to berate me in front of all the people.

'Late as always! I don't understand what could be more important than the meeting. Please come in and take a seat,' KK snorted like an angry bull on a rampage.

I looked around hoping to spot Subbu. I had to collect the list of programs from him.

Subbu was sitting in the far corner. He seemed to be enjoying my discomfort. He had his head down, as if writing something into the notebook, but I could make out the outline of a smile on his face.

I started moving in Subbu's direction hoping to find an empty seat close by.

'Why don't you sit in the vacant seat next to Arun?' suggested KK still sounding very angry.

I gulped before unwillingly taking the seat.

I wondered what AM was doing in our team meeting when he was not a member of our team.

The thought that he might be joining our team made me shudder. To report to AM was the last thing I wanted.

A bead of sweat trickled down my back as I sat on the chair.

My heart was beating fast as I worried about what lay in store for me.

'So, as I mentioned, there are batch report modules that can be tested independently without any dependencies. We will target them first before moving on to other modules. Anup, can I have the list please?' said KK looking at me.

In the world of mainframes modules can be broadly classified into two types, online and batch. In simple words online modules are interactive and usually need screens to read and display the results. The online modules also have a dependency on other online modules to complete the tasks they do. This limitation of online modules mean that they can be tested only when the screens are available and in certain cases when other online modules are ready.

The batch modules on the other hand are usually independent in nature. They are mainly used for generating reports or taking backups. Though the batch modules in certain cases may have a dependency on other modules, they can, mostly be tested independently.

KK's task for me had been to find such batch modules that could be tested without any other dependency. This task not only required a good understanding of the underlying system but also needed one to analyse the component designs. I was sure that KK had assigned me with this task knowing well that I was going to falter. He probably was patting himself on his smartness at pushing me to a corner. Meanwhile, I looked up feeling dizzy. I found it hard to breathe as my throat suddenly went dry.

What I was experiencing was worse than the ragging sessions at college when we had stood completely exposed, vulnerable in front of our seniors.

I could feel beads of sweat trickling down my back as I twitched uncomfortably.

Time stood still.

The whole meeting room was watching and waiting for me to react.

I felt KK's and AM's eyes boring into me.

Then KK opened his mouth to say something when Subbu suddenly interrupted him.

'Anup, you forgot this at your desk,' he said, passing me the list of modules.

I heaved a sigh of relief wondering why Subbu had taken so long to react. If he was just trying to put me in a spot, I was sure to get even with him after the meeting.

I clenched my teeth as I stood up to collect the list from Subbu. I handed the list to KK without bothering to look at them, which probably was a mistake. Knowing Subbu, you could never be sure when he was about to pull a prank on you.

Thankfully for me, Subbu was not in his prankster mode today.

KK glanced through the list, reading out few of the modules before asking me to include the list in one of his spreadsheets so that everyone could refer to it. I thanked my stars. I could have kissed Subbu for the favour.

Subbu deserved all the drinks I could buy for him at Shiva's.

Then I sank back heavily into my seat. My heart was trying to break free from the rib cage.

I was so relieved that I lost focus during the rest of the meeting. I was back to dreaming about my recent tryst with Rajni. I wondered how it would feel to be married to Rajni. I was oblivious to what was happening around me. I was in London with her when I was suddenly brought back to the meeting room. I noticed that everyone was looking at me expectantly again.

I shuddered wondering what KK had conjured up this time.

'Anup, can we please have your updates?' repeated KK, as I continued to stare blankly wondering what had hit me.

'I . . . umm,' I was trying hard to remember what I had done that week.

I could recollect nothing worthy of being mentioned in the meeting. But that reply would annoy KK even further.

'I have started coding the JP Modules,' I managed, recollecting the cryptic component designs I had been struggling with before my meeting with Rajni.

'How many modules have you completed?' asked KK.

'I have finished one and am working on two more,' I replied, not knowing what else to say.

'Have you tested it?' asked KK.

It seemed like KK was determined to eradicate me from the planet!

I had to continue building on my lies. I had to make it convincing enough to save myself from extermination.

I wondered what Rajni would do in London in my absence.

I quickly brought my thoughts back to the present knowing well that I had to act fast. I was really having a bad day, and no one could save me now.

'I have tested it with a stub module but am waiting for Chetan to complete his module before I can complete my testing.' I hoped Bhau would not ask me to volunteer the name of the module.

Thankfully, Bhau was too busy writing notes to have heard me.

The only reason I had mentioned Bhau's name was because I was sure KK would not go back to Bhau wanting to know the name of the module or the reason for the delay. KK was sure to be satisfied because if something was taking Bhau time it had to be very complicated.

My plan had worked!

KK seemed satisfied enough to move on to the next

person. I sank deeper into my chair, wishing I could completely vanish.

'Time for the updates,' said KK smiling, once everyone had provided him with their status.

Management updates were usually the last item on the agenda. They usually brought in a surprise element to the meeting. It also provided KK with an opportunity to stamp his superiority over us since he learnt about the new developments much before us.

KK cleared his throat before starting.

I noticed that AM had a smile on his face and was nodding in agreement to what KK had to say. This meant that KK had shared updates with him before the meeting. I padded myself hoping this would signal the end of my troubles at the meeting.

I looked up at KK eagerly, hoping that my enthusiasm would placate his ego enough for him to let me be in peace till the next meeting.

'There are many new developments this week,' KK added before pausing. Then he looked around to see whether his words had the desired effect on us.

Having satisfied himself, KK continued, 'I have been asked to take on a bigger role along with my current set of responsibilities. I know it is going to be hard on you people because I will be spending less time with you. I might not be able to give you the individual attention that I was earlier able to. The organization is growing and it needs me to take on more tasks. You know how I have always strived to meet my commitments, and there is no way I could refuse now when they are banking on my skills,' KK had a wide smile on his face as he completed the last sentence.

I think that managers around the world are trained in how to paint a rosy picture about the organization they work in and about themselves, sugar-coating the bitter pill and then feeding them to the ignorant lower levels. The poor souls who make up the labour force of an IT industry, swallow these pills, blissfully assuming that the managers are always right. A few smart ones who are brave enough to question the decisions end up paying for their arrogance, while the smartest of the lower rungs keep mum knowing well that it would hamper their chances to grow if they questioned the manager. A few name this art of keeping mum or agreeing to the manager as sycophancy or buttering but honestly it is the smartest thing to do.

I was unsure about what KK had said—I wondered whether the news was good or bad. KK leaving the team would surely mean fewer spreadsheets and less prodding. I did not think we would miss him very much. But there was more and I pulled my thoughts back, trying to concentrate on what he was saying.

KK continued 'I am very happy that the organization has listened and agreed to my request. They have assigned Arun to our team. Arun will help me in managing the team. He will be sharing my responsibilities so that I would be left with more time for the new projects.'

Now, that explained our being blessed with the divine presence of AM in the cafeteria and the meeting room!

There was really no good choice between KK with his spreadsheets and the conceited, toadying AM, but my vote would have gone to KK, with his spreadsheets included.

'I would also like to announce that we have a new employee on the team,' KK continued. 'Aman Sharma will be joining our team tomorrow.'

We spent the next few minutes in Austin before the meeting was finally adjourned. I rushed to the coffee machine, hoping to catch a glimpse of Rajni. Unfortunately, she had already left for the day. I could not see her handbag at her desk.

I waited for Subbu and Parag to collect their coffee as we stood around discussing the events at the meeting while we waited for Bhau to join us.

Coffee machines provide employees with a common point to meet and discuss their troubles and the private lives of their colleagues. They also act as stress busters; being placed at a distance from the workstations, they provide employees with a good walk. Coffee machines are the 'balance' part of 'Work Life Balance' equations.

A member of higher management near coffee machines is an unusual sight. A manager near coffee machines can only mean one of the two things, he is either trying to sweet-talk you into something to meet his ends or he is eavesdropping on his subordinates. A manager around coffee machines might confuse a few ignorant employees which can be dangerous. The ignorant employees believe that the manager is trying to socialize. They start trusting the manager and end up spilling the beans. Such employees are a great help for the manager in accomplishing his spying missions. Managers love such employees and usually keep a few of them in the team, even if it means that the other members are hard pressed to deliver because of the deficiencies of the manager's favourite lot.

'Bhau is not at his desk,' said Subbu walking back towards the coffee machine. We had waited for him in vain before Subbu had decided to check out his seat.

'I guess Bhau is held up in some discussion with KK,' said Parag.

We decided to go down to the cafeteria without Bhau. We knew he would join us when he got back. Till then, Subbu, Parag and I could sit with our coffee and mull over our troubles.

4

THE BLUE WORLD

When we returned from our coffee break, we found Bhau sitting at his desk, staring morosely at his computer screen.

I had never seen Bhau so sad.

His research lab seemed to have closed shop: there was no clicking of keys, the cursor stood blinking against the black background waiting for the next instruction. The drone of the fan trying to cool the computer could be heard against the silence.

Only an occasional click far away reminded us that we were not alone in the office.

~

The office usually emptied by six every evening, but a few employees stayed late after others had left. These were ones who were overloaded with work; or in a few cases it was only incompetence. Some even stayed back because there was nothing to go back to after office hours and to avail of the endless coffees, the air-conditioning and a free dinner. There were also some who did not leave at six because they wanted their superiors to appreciate and recognize their presence at these late hours.

Time differences between work locations and work cultures were other reasons for employees to stay back after office hours. An Indian employee supporting work in America tended to stay longer in office compared to the one who supported clients in Europe.

Bhau stayed back because he could not bear to leave a task incomplete. An incomplete task gnawed at him throughout the night allowing him only a fitful sleep. And also, because he loved what he did.

In other parts of the world Bhau would have made millions had he gone contracting or at least aspired to become a technical expert for the organization he worked in. In India there was only one way Bhau could go, which was to grow vertically. He would either become a good manager or die trying to understand why he could not.

Subbu walked over to Bhau's cubicle and sat on his desk, next to the computer. I joined him and Parag followed us. The four of us had been inseparable since the time we had joined the organization. We had gone through the good and the not so good times together, standing by each other. Our relationship had only become stronger.

'Let's go to Shiva's today?' suggested Bhau.

Bhau's face looked as if it had aged several years between the time we had the meeting and now. I noticed his eyes glisten with moisture. A feeling of emptiness rose within me.

I stood there feeling helpless. I wondered if I could ever aspire to get promoted. I shuddered at the thought of innumerable questions that life had in store for me. I feared that the answers to these questions were not what I had wanted them to be. It was not so much the fear of failure that troubled me, what I was more scared of was the knowledge that I did not deserve the results I wished for.

I suddenly remembered one of our good times together when we had gone to Jaipur on a weekend trip. The four of us had hired a cab to go to the pink city. Parag loved sleeping, and we knew, if left to himself, we wouldn't be able to leave the house before noon. Subbu and Bhau stayed at Parag's flat that night in order to ensure that we weren't delayed. They probably had beaten drums to get Parag to wake up and get ready in time for us to start. At least that is what I thought until, a good hundred miles into the trip, we discovered that Parag's fiancée to be lived in Jaipur! That explained our early start and Parag's eagerness to get moving.

We reached Jaipur around noon. On the way we had stopped at a small dhaba and devoured the sumptuous aloo and gobi paranthas. We decided to explore the city for a few hours before stopping for lunch.

It was around two in the afternoon when we checked into a hotel called the Broadway Inn. The only good thing about the hotel was that it fit our budget. The rooms had the bare essentials and I was relieved that the bedspread and the towels were clean unlike other hotels I had been to during our college trips. There were two beds separated by a small stool with an old table lamp on it. There were also two chairs and a small centre table. The rooms had a balcony that opened to the view of a busy Jaipur road.

Parag and I shared a room while Bhau and Subbu took the other room. We had brought along a bottle of Bacardi and packs of cards and all we needed was a bottle of coke to get started. Parag and I immediately took to the streets after having checked in. We were looking for cigarettes and a two litre bottle of Coke. Meanwhile Subbu and Bhau set about unpacking their stuff and getting the room ready for a game of cards. It took us a good thirty minutes to find a shop that sold a two litre bottle of Coke. It is really funny how things suddenly become elusive when you are looking for them. The sun was scorching bright, and we wanted to get back to the room as quickly as possible.

Every trip we had gone on together had ended up in a similar fashion—the four of us, a bottle of Bacardi-Reserva with Coke, and a pack of cards was all that we needed to have the time of our lives.

'Subbu it's your turn to shuffle the cards now,' I said, feeling a little tipsy from all the drinking. While trying to shuffle the cards he dropped the deck on the floor. We spent the next few minutes, picking up the cards which seemed like quite a task for we were all a little drunk. Crouching on your knees while trying to pick plastic cards from the floor is tougher than you think once you have had a few drinks!

'You clumsy idiot!' shouted Parag, annoyed at having to pick the cards.

Parag was tall, dark and well built. He was the most handsome member of our group and probably the most intelligent too. His sculpted look enhanced his features making him look mature. He was the kind of guy whom you could love and trust with your life. Perhaps that is why I had opened up to him. That he was physically strong was a well-known fact too—he had once twisted Subbu's arm in anger when they had had a scuffle. Subbu's

arm had continued to pain for two days and since then he
had refrained from trying anything smart on Parag.

Subbu meekly went on picking up the cards. Bhau and
I smiled at each other relishing Subbu's discomfort.

As we continued to play Bhau did well to maintain his
losing streak. He downed one drink after another in order
to bolster himself after every defeat. The drinks failed to
revive his luck but they did help him in forgetting the
previous loss.

The bottle was almost empty when Bhau dropped on
the bed and curled up in a foetal position.

Parag, Subbu and I broke into peals of laughter looking
at Bhau in the compromising position. He had a blissful
smile on his face and was in a deep sleep, unaware of the
world around him.

'I am not sharing this room with him!' shouted Subbu.

'Get me a matchbox! I am going to light him up!' said
Parag excitedly, enjoying his own joke. 'He has enough
alcohol inside him to make him go flying out of the
window!'

Bhau was oblivious to the activity around him.

Subbu, Parag and I walked out to the balcony for a
smoke. We were feeling happy and free from all our
worries, we laughed at everything around us, even the
silliest of jokes managed to tickle us to death.

There was a lone chair in the corner of the balcony. On
the opposite end ran a waist high iron railing. I plopped
myself on the chair while Subbu and Parag leaned against
the railing. The road below was slowly coming to life as
the afternoon sun, having completed its day's toil, had
decided to go elsewhere. The pink city breathed a sigh of
relief as the temperature came down. There were people

walking with loads on their heads. There were cycle rickshaws, autos and carts moving alongside on the road. There were scooters, cars and bikes that were trying to squeeze through the medley of activity.

I noticed a man wearing a bright florescent green shirt and a pink pair of pants and I laughed uncontrollably pointing towards the man as Subbu and Parag looked at me perplexed.

'Imagine Subbu wearing those!' I managed before going back to my uncontrolled laughing. Subbu grimaced a little before joining in our merriment. He probably thought that the pink pants could have been a little brighter.

We were having one of the best times of our lives.

It was always the same every time the four of us drank together. We were transported to a different planet. A world of our own, where there was no one to judge or deny us anything that we wished for. It was a world where Rajni, AM, KK, Mom and Dad took a back seat. They did not completely disappear, but were temporarily moved to a corner, at the back of our minds, waiting there for the alcohol to lose its effect.

These drinking frenzies were our way of rebelling against the world we lived in. They were my answers to the questions I did not want to face or could not resolve.

Subbu drank because it helped him run away from memories.

Bhau drank to forget that the world was not fair, being always skewed in favour of a lucky few.

Parag drank to enjoy a little more of life.

Whichever way, we were running away from our troubles and worries. Running away because we were frightened. We were cowards in disguise, trying to put up a brave front for the external world. We were frightened to speak our minds to the likes of KK and AM.

We were stuck in our islands of comfort worrying that there was no land across seas. We were scurrying around looking for cheese that we did not wish to eat. We were punishing ourselves because that is where we thought our redemption lay.

People would call us a bunch of losers, they could even laugh at us, but did we care?

Looking back at those times, our troubles seemed to exist only in our minds, all that we needed to do was to face them, but no one was going to teach us how. No one told us because no one knew the answers; everyone was busy running away from their troubles. Each one of them had their own demons to fend off, scurrying away from change.

We sat there in the balcony for a long time looking at the traffic.

An alarm brought us back to the real world and action. It was five o'clock. I ordered some tea for all of us while Subbu got to work cleaning the room. You could not help but admire Subbu at times like this. He was like a mother who cared little for the toil she put in for her children's sake. He acted without desire for a reward or recognition.

We sat sipping our tea.

Bhau was still asleep. The smile on his face had been replaced by a frown. He was probably having a bad dream. Subbu had tried without success to wake him for a cup of tea.

'We would have to leave in an hour's time to get to Chowki Dhani,' said Parag.

5

AT SHIVA'S

'Let's go to Shiva's today,' suggested Bhau.

Subbu's eyes twinkled as he heard the name of his favourite pub.

Parag and I had nothing better to do that day.

I did not want to go back to my desk after the unpleasant experience at the team meeting. I was sure that a drink or two would help calm my nerves and put things into perspective.

There was a lot of work to be done but it would have to wait till tomorrow.

~

I had to drop the car at Dad's office before we could go to Shiva's. Generally, I avoided going home after our drinking sprees. I was sure Mom and Dad knew that I had an occasional drink or two, but when we were at Shiva's, there was no stopping us. Also, I avoided driving when drunk, preferring to stay back at Parag's, Bhau's or Subbu's flat.

It was decided that Parag and I would go and leave the

car at Dad's office while Subbu and Bhau finished up things at work.

We agreed to meet at Shiva's in an hour.

Among the four of us we shared a single bike which was owned by Bhau. Neither Parag nor Subbu had a vehicle. It was an old model which was in great condition because of Bhau's constant care and attention. His father had bought it a few years before his retirement. Bhau prized the bike more than any gift he had ever received. Naturally, he hated loaning his bike though he did make an exception at times by allowing Parag the privilege; for others, which included Subbu and me, the bike was out of bounds. When Parag and I saw off Subbu he was busy hunting with his microscope, checking his desk for unwanted stuff to be shredded.

I got the Santro out of the parking lot, and waited for Parag who pulled up beside the car on Bhau's bike a few minutes later.

'Chalo, else we will be late. The traffic looks really bad. I will also need to stop over at Shoppers Stop on the way back. I have to get Rajni a gift for her birthday.'

Parag raised his eyebrows at me before wearing the helmet.

The roads where chock-a-block with cars and bikes. It took us thirty minutes to cover three miles to Dad's office. I went in to hand over the car keys to him. He seemed to be busy with work, finishing up for the day, and momentarily glanced up at me to take the keys before immersing himself back into the work.

'Enjoy within limits!' he said huffily before getting back to whatever he was doing.

'No Dad, I have a lot of work to do,' I said, knowing

fully well that he could see right through me. However, before long I was thinking about the gift I was going to get Rajni for her birthday.

Parag slowed the bike as we neared Shoppers Stop. The mall was just beginning to fill up.

I always preferred getting Rajni a dress or something that she could wear. I guess my choice of gifts was primarily because I was a Capricorn. I had read so much about the general traits of people belonging to Capricorn and Taurus that I had most of the facts by heart.

The advantage with Shoppers Stop was that it was in between Shiva's and Dad's place of work.

Parag busied himself at the music store next door while I headed towards the ladies section to find Rajni a gift. Parag hated spending time in the ladies section.

～

It had been twenty minutes since I had walked into the shop but was still unable to find a dress that caught my fancy. Then I spotted a red shirt on the new arrivals section. I started walking towards it to take a closer look, when my eyes wandered over to the lingerie section. I felt a little uncomfortable and immediately looked away.

I passed a group of girls who were busy admiring a pale blue top. The girls looked up at me and whispered something, before breaking into giggles.

I quickened my steps wanting to finish the shopping as quickly as possible.

I remembered the time when I had visited Shoppers Stop with Rajni. She had wanted to get a birthday gift for Payal. At that time she had allowed me to accompany her because she needed someone to drive her down, and since I had a car I qualified.

I had known Rajni only for a few months then. It was much before I had·fallen for her. I had been very proud that day to be walking the aisles of the store with a beautiful girl and wondered what the people watching us made of Rajni and me. That was the first time when I felt an urge to touch Rajni and feel her close to me.

It all seemed to have happened in the long past. In the year between then and now a lot had changed. Rajni and I had shared our feelings for each other. We were now so much a part of each other's life that it was hard to imagine otherwise. At least, that is how I felt about our relationship.

Once Rajni and I had realized that we were in love, we had stopped frequenting crowded places. There was something within us that had changed. We felt insecure in public. We thought that everyone who saw us immediately knew that we were in love.

I pulled the red shirt from the shelf for close inspection. It had black checks against a red background and I was at once sure that it would look beautiful on Rajni. The red colour would accentuate her fair complexion, especially when she would blush. Happy that I had finally found what I had wanted, I fruitlessly rummaged through the shelves for a size that would fit her.

I was still searching when the sales assistant approached me.

'Can I help you sir?' she volunteered.

I looked up feeling a little awkward.

'I am looking for a medium size,' I said pointing at the shirt.

The sales assistant spent time going through all the shelves that I had just finished looking at, before turning to me and apologizing. It is frustrating when you spend hours looking for something you like, and finally when you find it, the store does not have the size you need.

'Sir I think we might have some pieces in the store room,' she said looking at my crestfallen face. 'Will you please wait, while I confirm it for you?'

I stood there looking around and praying that she would have the shirt when she returned.

However, my prayers went unanswered when I saw her come back empty-handed. I grimaced before readying myself to start my search afresh but the sales assistant interrupted my thoughts.

'Sir, we might have the size and the pattern you are looking for in a dark shade of blue,' she said. I reluctantly agreed to take a look. A few minutes later I was standing at the billing counter paying for the dark blue shirt, still wishing that I had been able to buy the red one.

I wonder how things would have turned out if I had bought the red shirt instead, but like so many other things in life, I will never know the answer. Rajni never learnt about the red shirt and always thought that the dark blue one had been my first choice.

She was wearing the blue shirt when she got a promotion.

Rajni was wearing the blue shirt when she severed a relationship that she had cherished for years—a relationship that probably would never be the same again.

I have my memories of her in the blue shirt, some of which I would cherish and some that I would love to forget. But I will always wonder how things would have turned out if it had been the red shirt. Would our fates have been different?

~

I found Parag sitting on the wooden seat near McDonalds. He was busy eating a burger.

'I am sorry,' I said apologizing for the delay.

Parag smiled. It was nearly eight in the evening. We walked towards the parking to pick the bike and drive down to Shiva's. The roads were empty by then and it took us only about ten minutes to reach.

~

Shiva's was what one called a poor man's pub, unlike those high-end market pubs that had started sprouting around Delhi recently. It was a place where you could get drinks at affordable rates without having to bother with the happy hours and the innumerable taxes that the big shops charged. It was a small restaurant, more like a dhaba, which had sprouted next to a 'Wine and Beer' shop. It not only served good, cheap food but also allowed connoisseurs such as us to carry drinks in from the 'Wine and Beer' store next door. A good *jugaad*, a win-win arrangement for both the restaurant and the beer store!

When we reached, Subbu and Bhau were waiting for us at a corner table. As soon as he saw us Subbu got into action, 'I am going to buy four bottles of Tempest cider.' Parag and I took seats next to Bhau and waited for the drinks to arrive.

Around us were plain walls covered by a simple asbestos sheet for a roof. The liquor shop was separated from the rest of the building by an iron grille. There was a small opening in the iron grille that served as a counter. A small rectangular table near the entrance served grilled meat and a tandoor was placed adjacent to it. Inside the restaurant, at the far end, there was a small room that served as a kitchen for vegetarian dishes which included eggs. There were a set of rickety fans that hung from the asbestos roof.

The only purpose these fans served was to create a constant drone reminding one of their mundane existence.

Inside the restaurant there were two rows of plastic tables and chairs with an aisle in between. There were about twelve tables. Each table had roughly six chairs around it. On Fridays and weekends it was hard to find an empty seat in Shiva's.

Bhau had still not recovered since the meeting.

He looked across at me and Parag morosely, 'I will not get promoted this year,' he said to no one in particular. His voice was full of resentment, the finality of defeat. Parag and I looked at each other not knowing how to react. Thankfully, Subbu returned a few seconds later with the bottles, easing the tension.

'Why do you say that? Is it because AM has joined our team now?' asked Parag.

'Yes, but it is not just AM. I hear that Aman Sharma, the new guy, is joining as a team leader. This could only mean that they are not going to promote me,' said Bhau.

Bhau's speculation was justified.

Every year, around the time for the annual reviews, there seemed to be a lot of uncertainty at office. It was one of the most dreaded periods of the year. Apart from having to fend for what one thought he or she rightly deserved, at the one-on-one sessions with managers, one also had to brace himself for the final results. The organization never seemed to live up to either the hype or the employee expectations.

This year the rumour mills had predicted very few promotions and lower hikes than last year. The reason being the global recession. Our company was doing particularly badly and had been a takeover target for a few months before the appraisal, making us glad that we at least had our jobs!

It was widely known that if you are a part of an organization that gets taken over, you always lose out in the bargain. According to me most IT companies were doing badly, not because of the markets but because of the aggressive targets they set for themselves. The media and the press played a very important role too; they always provided higher footage to the losers and the losses.

I still remember the only time when our organization had distributed huge bonuses for the profits they had made in the previous quarter. They had ended up turning a few heads, but it all seems like a fantasy now.

In the normal course there were always a few promotions, a few hikes and some heartbreaks. The mood in office was at its lowest during such periods. The employees who got the better of the bargain were unhappy because they wanted more while the employees who had lost out thought they deserved more.

Bhau had been hoping for a promotion this year but looking at the recent changes in the team, he did not fancy his chances.

'But you love coding! Why would you want to get promoted?' asked Subbu as he took another gulp from his bottle.

Though Subbu had a very simplistic view of everything, he was right. But in this industry it was never that simple. And each of us had our own way of dealing with such things.

'Why are the snacks taking such a long time? I think I need to check,' said Parag, getting up. I recalled he had just eaten at McDonalds. Was he was really hungry or was it just an excuse to move away from the table and the conversation?

Parag believed that the annual appraisal was a fruitless exercise.

Indian IT industry still believes in experience-linked promotions. You are promoted only if you have spent the required number of years in the organization. If you get promoted after having spent the required number of years, it is normal, but if you fail you are regarded as incompetent.

Though things are changing, they are happening very slowly, sometimes in the right direction and sometimes for the worse. Nobody wants to accept mistakes and make amends. Nobody wants the change. It's like Indians playing cricket with baseball equipment!

Subbu returned with a round of drinks.

'Hey, what have you got inside the Shoppers Stop bag? Must be a gift for your girl, isn't it? Let me tell you, you are a big doormat!' he said before breaking into peals of laughter.

Parag and Bhau joined in, forgetting the discussion we were having.

'Oh, what did you get her this time? Is it a diamond necklace?' continued Subbu, laughingly.

My phone suddenly started vibrating with frenzy. It probably wanted to take down Subbu.

'Rajni calling' it said before going silent.

Rajni was giving me a missed call, which meant that she was free to take a call from me. Given the latest comment, I resisted my temptation to walk out and call her. I sat there waiting for the right moment.

The phone rang again, but this time it continued to ring for a while. Rajni had probably assumed that I had missed her previous call.

This time I walked out of the restaurant before dialling her number.

'I am so sorry, dear,' said Rajni answering my call on

the very first ring. 'I was so busy today. So what are you doing?' she asked before I could answer.

I could never understand Rajni, she could sometimes be very loving and caring and at times turn into someone who hardly knew me.

'I am with Parag and Bhau at a restaurant,' I answered, not wanting to mention Subbu knowing well how much Rajni hated him.

'Is Subbu not there? I am sure you guys are drinking.'

'Nahi baba,' I said in reply to her question. 'I've just had one beer,' I added, realizing that I was not going to succeed in lying to Rajni.

She somehow always managed to find out the truth. I think it was my voice that gave me away.

'You are impossible! I ask you for one thing, and you don't even do that for me. How long have I been asking you to stop drinking?' she said, sounding concerned in her best melodramatic tone.

I think acting concerned was probably just one of her ways of showing that she cared. I did not mind, because I loved it when she did that.

Rajni and I spoke for a few more minutes before she had to hang up as her Mom had returned home from the market.

'Love you,' she had whispered before disconnecting the call. I was sure no alcohol could have made me feel as high as I felt right then.

Meanwhile oblivious to my predicament, Subbu had brought in a third set of drinks. I quickly gulped down what was left of my second one before starting on the third.

'Was it Rajni?'

I nodded.

'Oh boy, you are pathetic!' said Subbu, with a wry smile. That was enough to set me off.

'Shut up, Subbu! There are other people around. I don't want them to hear. Please keep quiet,' I retorted angrily.

'Oh, the lover boy is angry. What do you people think? I am sure everyone in office knows by now,' added Subbu.

I was beginning to feel miserable.

Parag, fathoming my discomfort, asked Subbu out for a smoke.

I looked at Bhau. He was staring at the wall.

6

THANK GOD IT'S FRIDAY

My head was still pounding from all the drinking and lack of sleep when I got into office on Friday. Bhau and Subbu were already at their desks when Parag and I walked in.

The office did not feel the same today.

I knew Rajni wasn't coming in and it frustrated me no end to think that I would not be able to give her a call to wish her on her birthday. A strange kind of emptiness engulfed me making me feel uneasy and restless. My heart felt heavy. I wondered what she was doing as I placed the Shoppers Stop bag into the drawer at my desk.

I felt a huge urge to peep inside the bag and to take another look at the gift I had bought. And I looked around towards Subbu's cubicle to make sure that he was not watching me before slowly pulling the blue shirt out from the bag and holding it in my hands. I wondered how my Rajni would look when she wore it. It would be Monday before I would get an opportunity to see her.

'Doormat!' hissed Subbu suddenly appearing from nowhere. I replied by staring hard right back at him, before hurriedly putting the shirt back into the bag and dropping it into the drawer.

'It is Rajni's birthday. She is turning twenty-four today,' I said, hoping that sharing my thoughts with Subbu would help me deal with the loneliness that I had suddenly felt.

As I clicked on the Outlook icon to bring up the mailbox, I had the overwhelming feeling of being one amongst the thousands of people working in IT and other industries all around the world, who check their emails first thing in the morning.

There were a few emails from my friends Ravi, Kareem and Pradeep. There was an email chain doing rounds, with everyone replying to everyone; they probably had found some new topic to discuss about. The emails were about the forthcoming marriage of a friend, where everyone was trying to pull his leg. There had been quite a few marriages in our circle. All my friends seemed to be tying the knot one after the other.

The last email had been from Kareem.

Kareem was still working with my previous organization in Bangalore. We had last met at Neeraj's wedding. Neeraj had soon slipped out of our mailing group and the chain mails but Kareem and I had stayed in touch. We would often discuss how Neeraj had changed since his marriage and assumed that the additional responsibility was getting to him; or was it that he did not find much to interest him in our childish mails.

Kareem Mohammad would soon be leaving for the United States. He was very excited about his new assignment. The happenings around the world did make things a little tough for him but that did not dampen his enthusiasm.

I recollected how we had all visited Kareem at his

house during Id, a few years ago when I was still living in Bangalore. The thought of the wonderful biryani Kareem's ammi had prepared that day, still made my mouth water.

'To hell with the suckers—we need to do better next time,' Kareem's reply had read.

I scrolled down trying to get an idea of what was being discussed. It had something to do with the match between India and Australia.

I wondered what our lives would have been without the mobiles and emails that we are now addicted to. I spend at least an hour each day replying to emails.

There was an email from AM at the bottom of the pile. I clicked on it.

It was a meeting invite.

'1–1 meeting,' read the subject line.

I accepted the invitation, wondering what new game was about to be played with us tortured souls.

I turned towards Subbu.

'Yes, I too have an invitation from AM for a one-on-one meeting,' said Subbu reading my thoughts.

Getting a meeting invite from AM was never a good sign, if you were Subbu or me.

The frown on my face told the story.

'Come on! Let's go to the canteen and get a bite. I am famished,' I suggested.

I followed the others, indifferent to the route they took. Rajni wasn't coming in anyway!

'What do you think AM wants from us?' I asked once we had picked up something to eat from the counter and found an empty table to sit.

Subbu was busy nibbling at his chocolate bar. It was amazing how many sweets Subbu could eat at any time of the day! There was a standing bet among us that he could eat a bar of chocolate with equal relish even when woken up in mid-sleep in the middle of the night.

'He probably wants to let us know how great he is,' put in Parag.

'He probably wants to console me for not getting the promotion,' added Bhau. We grimaced. There was little that we would hear from Bhau for the next few days if not months.

I was disturbed: 'He should spend some time with the team first and try to understand what is going on. You need to give people time to settle down and understand the change. You don't jump into a new team and start sending out invites for 1–1 meetings!' I said expressing my outrage, or was it panic?

'Oh, now you are going to teach Mr AM how to work, are you?' asked Parag, smiling.

While we were walking back to our desks, I noticed that AM had moved into the empty cubicle next to where KK sat and now they were having an animated discussion with someone whom we had never seen before. I looked at the trio a little longer trying to recognize the new face before finally giving up and walking back to my seat.

I had just logged on to my computer when AM walked up to my desk with the new person we had earlier seen at KK's desk.

'Hi Anup! This is Aman Sharma. Aman will be joining our team. He is new to the organization, so he will shadow me for a while before he takes up the new responsibilities. I hope you will help him settle in,' said AM rushing through the introductions.

'Hi, Aman,' I managed to smile.

AM always acted very busy, he always seemed to be short of time as if trying to catch the last flight out of the city. I never could figure out if he was just putting on an act or if he was really that busy. Whatever it was, he sure had a way of making everyone around him feel insignificant. I think it was the craftiness of a jackal combined with the sleaziness of a snake that combined in AM's nature.

I suddenly remembered what my mother had once said, 'Son, you can trust snakes in a jungle, but never trust people who are crafty.'

Once he completed the introduction, AM immediately turned around and headed to Subbu's seat. He literally pulled Aman away from my desk. Aman and I had not even got a chance to exchange pleasantries.

I noticed Aman shrugging his shoulders and smiling at me before leaving my desk.

I felt sorry for Aman.

From then on AM acted like a shield protecting Aman from us for the rest of the day. He took him everywhere he went.

Subbu observed, 'They probably went to the loo together too. Guess now we have twins to fight instead of just AM.' Parag laughed out loud but I did not find it so funny.

There was little we could do.

~

We had a quiet lunch that afternoon before getting back to work. There was the 1–1 meeting with AM to deal with. I checked my mobile for the nth time that day, hoping for a missed call from Rajni, letting me know that I could call her. Unfortunately, there wasn't any. The day was taking a turn for the worse. I got back to my desk and started answering emails from my friends. Srinivas, my friend from college who had joined an IT company in Chennai, wanted to know how I was placed for the weekend. He told me Ravi, who was a mutual friend from college, was coming down from Chennai and was hoping that I could meet him on Saturday. There were a few more emails from my other friends that I replied to before getting bored and deciding to catch up on my work.

I was midway into coding a module when a reminder popped up, warning me about the impending meeting with AM. I immediately stopped what I was doing and started preparing for it. I did not want to get late for my first meeting with AM because the last thing I wanted from Mr Know-it-all was a lecture about being late for meetings.

I reached Austin with time to spare and anxiously waited outside the meeting room. Subbu was inside with AM.

Subbu's meeting with AM was scheduled to start an hour and half before mine. They had been inside the room for a little more than an hour. I wondered what they were discussing. I had an urge to listen into their conversation. Just minutes later Subbu walked out with a frown on his face. Obviously their discussion had not been a very pleasant one. He seemed to be seething with anger. This made me even more nervous.

I knocked on the door before waiting for AM to summon me.

As I walked in I noticed AM sitting on one corner of the rectangular table, while Aman sat beside him taking notes.

'Ah, Anup, come in and have a seat. You did not bring your diary, did you?' asked AM sounding very much in his element—the conceited creep! He was a master at making you feel incompetent. The meeting had started badly for me and AM now had me at his mercy. I felt that not bringing the diary along was the biggest mistake I had ever made in my entire life! AM loved pushing people into a corner before he started any meeting. He was a leech that survived by sucking co-workers' blood. It was my turn today.

I had been unlucky to have my meeting scheduled after Subbu's. I am sure AM had tasted blood and was now looking for a kill. I uttered my prayers hoping that the gods would have mercy on me.

I missed KK and his spreadsheets. He was God when compared to AM.

All of a sudden, it dawned on me—everything is relative!

I guess at times like this letting your thoughts wander away from the situation you are in helps you tap the hidden courage and face the onslaught of whatever it is you are against.

I would probably never completely understand my thoughts, but who could blame me for my confusion? By then I was feeling light and easy, and ready to handle whatever AM had in store for me.

I guess looking death in its face does that to people.

'Arun, I thought it was a 1–1,' I said harnessing my newly discovered courage.

The second biggest mistake one could ever make with people like AM was to tell them that they were wrong. It probably would have been smarter to kick myself in the gut. I felt like vomiting all over Austin and AM. What was I doing? Trying to kill myself!

The next fifteen minutes were spent on learning and relearning corporate ethics and meeting etiquettes. I was looking for a way to run out of the meeting. I was feeling claustrophobic.

'I have received a lot of bad reviews about you, Anup,' continued AM. He waited for his words to sink in. He waited until the colour had drained from my face before continuing.

'I really doubt if you will even get a hike this time. If this feedback was sent to Human Resources they would probably ask you to leave the organization,' AM added.

By now I was completely thrown over. Everything he said seemed to pass by me without registering. I dreaded the thought of being left without a job. At this stage there weren't many options I could think of. I wondered if Rajni would ever agree to marry me if I was left without a job. I am sure I made a pretty sight sitting there helplessly, conjuring up pictures of the plight that would befall me if HR decided to render me jobless.

AM waited for what felt like hours before he continued, 'I am not like other managers. I have my standards and ways of judging. I knew from the first time we had met in the cafeteria, that you had a lot of potential. All I need to do is to channelize it.' This came as a complete surprise to me after what I had heard AM say earlier.

What *did* this guy have in store for me now?

I could not help noticing the number of 'I's that were being thrown at me. AM sure was a conceited fellow.

'I am going to draw up a plan to help you tap your potential. I will monitor you on a weekly basis. I am sure we will prove all the others wrong,' added AM.

Was it all about proving others wrong? Did AM really

want to help me or was he trying to snub everyone in their face by helping me 'tap my potential'.

My head was spinning; I was feeling weak and wanted water before I fainted.

AM stood up, ready to leave the meeting room, but before opening the door, he added, 'I think you can be better than Chetan if you put your mind to it.'

What did AM mean by that? I wondered. I surely was not half as good as Bhau. For heavens, I was not even in the same league as he!

Bhau knew everything about the project we were working on. Nobody could deliver a successful project without his help.

Had AM gone insane? I hoped he had.

I sat there in the meeting room for a long time after AM had left, trying to collect myself. I was struggling not to break down and cry. I could not imagine having to inform Dad that I had been thrown out of the company. I was sure Dad would concur with everything AM had said. The only difference perhaps would be that he would wonder why the company had not kicked me out earlier!

I had been a good student at school. I had managed to scrape through college without having to redo any subject. I wasn't very smart, but I had always been above average. What had gone wrong with my life? I sat there wondering what Rajni would think if she heard all this.

Rajni would have been ashamed of me and rightly so. A wonderful girl like her deserved a better person.

I hated myself for having bought that gift for Rajni. I wondered if I was trying to buy her with my silly gifts. I probably was trying to win over something that I did not rightly deserve.

I knew Rajni could easily find a person, who was more suitable for her love. I was fooling myself and all the people around me. I was the loser who did not deserve the life he was living. I had never felt so low in my life.

I walked out of the meeting room, determined to make amends. I would make myself worthy of Rajni and my parents. I would work hard to earn the life that I had.

I would prove AM and everyone around me wrong.

7

JUST ANOTHER MANIC MONDAY—I

That Friday I went straight to bed without caring for dinner. Mom knocked endlessly on the door of my room and finally gave up. She was worried about me. Later that night I overheard my parents talking about my marriage. I wondered why lately everything I said or did got summarized into three simple words, 'get him married'. My aunts and uncles had only one question when they met me with my parents at family functions: 'When are you getting your son married?' Their concern for my betterment or what they thought was best for me troubled me endlessly.

Mom had been approached with a number of proposals for me. She had initially been polite with the refusals but had taken a different stance recently. I heard Mom mention to Dad about the latest proposal that had been referred to her: 'The girl is an engineer. She has done her master's from America,' my mother said sounding excited.

Yes, my mother had set a goal for herself, to get me married by the completion of the financial year. With every proposal she became more animated in her discussions and basked in the attention that was being showered on her by the prospective bride's family. With this engineer girl Mom thought she had finally found a proposal suitable for me.

'The girl is returning from America this weekend. Her parents had called up, and wanted us to meet them sometime next week,' I could sense the pride in my mother's voice as she described the girl.

I pulled the pillow around my ears and tried to concentrate on the other important things in my life.

I finally fell asleep thinking about how Rajni would look in the bridal attire.

The next day I felt a little better but I still remembered the 1–1 meeting from Friday though I had forgotten some of the details. My determination to change myself was still very strong. I spent the morning, logged on to the Internet, working on my CV and chatting to my friends in other companies. I knew I had to start afresh and look for new opportunities. A new start in a new organization would give me a clean slate and make it easier for me to prove my potential.

I would show that snotty AM what my true potential was!

I had been chatting with Neeraj who was in America working for a client. He was telling of the wonderful trips he and his wife had made to Niagara Falls and Disneyland. I wished it had been me and Rajni instead, in America.

It was midnoon when my phone rang.

The ringing stopped even before I had an opportunity to make an attempt to look for the phone. I rushed to the phone realizing that it could be Rajni.

Who else would give me a missed call on the weekend?

However, I did not feel like talking to Rajni or for that matter anyone. I wanted time to myself to work out my priorities. I wished Rajni had not called then, but still dialled her number, out of habit.

'Hi! How are you?' I heard her sweet voice on the other end.

'I am out shopping with my parents. They are at the grocery store buying things for the house. I just walked out so that I could talk to you,' added Rajni without waiting for my answer. She sounded very happy. I guess the birthday celebration with her parents had lived up to her expectations. I felt a little jealous at my not being a part of it.

I was still feeling very down from my experience on Friday.

'Hmm, good,' I replied in a tone that failed to hide my frustration.

'Wah! You keep complaining to me that I never call you on weekends. Now when I have finally managed to call, you sound so bored. This is the last time I am going to call you over the weekend,' Rajni replied trying to sound angry, but her giggling gave her away.

Ordinarily I would have been elated that Rajni had managed to call me over the weekend, but how could I explain to her that today was different? How could I make Rajni understand that my frustration was not because of her call but because of my own doing?

'You haven't still wished me for my birthday,' added Rajni sounding really concerned this time.

'Anyways, I need to leave now, I can see Dad at the checkout counter. Love you,' she whispered. Rajni probably thought that I was still angry with her for not having called me on her birthday.

'Happy birthday sweetheart and can you please repeat the last line for me?' I said having recovered from Friday's aftermath in a jiffy.

'Anup! Tum na!' said Rajni with feigned irritation . . .

'Love you, love you, love you,' she whispered before disconnecting the phone.

I stood still holding the phone in my hand, still trying to recover from the elated state that Rajni's call had taken me to.

I suddenly felt very happy.

~

That evening I drove Mom out for shopping. She was relieved that I had recovered from the foul mood. She had pestered me a few times for the reason behind my mood, but finally forgot all about it as she took to shopping. She had even hinted about the new marriage proposal she had shortlisted for me a few times, but finally stopped after finding no support from either me or Dad.

We returned home a happy family that evening. Come to think of it, I am not really sure about Dad and myself but Mom was very happy.

My parents had gone to bed after dinner while I watched the Saturday blockbuster on a movie channel.

The movie was about a man who was exceptionally intelligent, but was unhappy with life. He seemed to be unable to shake away his turbulent past and hence was afraid to trust people or get into relationships. He searched in vain for answers, spending time doing things that were not befitting his intelligence. Finally when he found himself on the verge of fame and material success, he realized, thanks to a friendly professor, that this wasn't his purpose of life! That money and fame would never make him happy.

The next day he walked out from his old life in search of the girl whom he had once loved. He drove down the highway looking for this girl who had loved him back and made him feel complete. The movie ended with a scene that showed the hero following his dream.

I had tears in my eyes by the time the movie finished.

I wondered if I was in any way unlike the hero. I too was still looking for my purpose in life. I realized that I was very close to achieving what I wanted to . . . I wanted to marry Rajni, I wanted to make her mine.

If Rajni's call had made me feel happy, the movie had completed the jigsaw puzzle that had been playing on my mind since Friday.

I finally found reason in my existence.

Feeling very happy I logged on to the computer to check my mails before going to bed. There were no new mails in the mailbox. Not having anything better to do I opened up a word document to type a lengthy mail to Rajni. Midway through the mail I found my thoughts carrying me elsewhere and before long, I found myself writing a story in blank verse:

He stood watching.
He was unmoved by the tears gushing from my eyes.
He stood stark naked. He was oblivious to the eyes that were staring at his manhood.
He stood still as the rain washed down, trickling down his body.
He had stood still in the scorching heat of the afternoon sun.

He stared down at the people passing by, defiantly ignoring their snobbish utterings.

I sat at his feet trying to find answers to my questions. I had to know why he had done what he had.

He had not tried to stop the chair from falling. The chair had slipped from under her feet. He had not held her fall when the noose tightened around her neck.

He had not attempted to console her or reason with her.

He had let her die.

She had died a slow death, asphyxiated by the remorse of a love unrestrained.

He did not stop her when she had lost her will to lust.

He had looked away when she came, engulfed with pain and joy that only true love could bring.

'We can never get married,' she had said, every time I tired kissing her wanting lips.

Each time that I took her into my embrace, she pulled away in vain.

'We can never get married,' was all she had for me.

The day I had brought her flowers, she had cried.

The day I had held her hand on the bus, she had cried.

The day I had walked her back from college, she had cried.

How little did she know that I lost a part of me, every time she cried?

'We can never get married,' was all that she had said.

I sat at his feet realizing how true her words had

been. She had worked at changing our destiny . . .
little by little every time she uttered those words.
It was getting darker and the rain had stopped.
I looked up at the statue of Lord Gomateswara for
the last time.
I was bidding farewell to the city, a city to which I
never intended to return.

By the time I logged off, it was the wee hours of the
morning. Even then I had logged off not because my
enthusiasm about writing had subsided, but because my
eyes had refused to cooperate.

Strangely my thoughts had been going back to Subbu
as I had penned the story.

The good thing about that night was that I realized
what I had always cherished; I knew what I really wanted
from my life. I had always wanted to become a writer. But
the dream had become smaller with every passing year at
school and finally died during the last years of college. My
parents' will had superseded my desire; they had wanted a
secure future—that my dream would not guarantee—for
their son. But they were not the only ones to be blamed
for my predicament, because to a certain degree my fear
about the uncertainty of my future as a writer also played
a part. And my dream got trampled in the more immediate
and accepted requirements of the hour.

I called up Parag and read out the story to him. Parag
was patient throughout the narration and after I finished
he told me that he liked it. We discussed, and he felt that
I did have a chance, even though a bleak one at the
moment, of making it as a writer.

This new ray of hope made me excited on that Sunday.
I even attempted talking Dad into reading my story. He

listened carefully and then just nodded his head before getting back to working on his files. I felt a little snubbed by Dad's reaction but was still too enthused to completely lose hope in my ability as a writer.

I couldn't wait till I showed my story to Rajni and in the process forgot that the next day was Monday. It was probably my first weekend in a long time when I did not catch the 'Monday fever'—which rose in direct proportion to its proximity to the end of Sunday.

I was buoyed by the prospect of sharing my story with Rajni, coupled with the fact that I was meeting her after three days—on Monday, I was eager to leave home for work!

However, once I was at my desk, working on the module assigned to me, the memory of the 1–1 rushed right back. I was still to check my mailbox when Subbu walked in and greeted me before taking his seat.

Bhau and Parag were yet to come in.

I found it impossible to go any further with the module, and secretly hoped that Bhau would be in soon. There was little I could do with the component design or the module without understanding the underlying application, and the only person who could help me with that was Bhau.

Bhau had single-handedly designed most of the application for the project. Bhau was like a messiah, a saviour for people like me, a helpdesk for all of us who were stuck with our modules. It was no miracle that Bhau was always surrounded with queries on all types of technical problems and needless to say, he loved to aid the needy!

I struggled a little longer before giving into desperation and clicking the Outlook icon. There were very few emails in the inbox. It seemed that all my friends were still to come into office after the weekend. I had nothing else to do. I resisted the temptation of moving away from my seat.

I sat there hoping that by just sitting at my desk I could will things to change. I hoped that sitting at the desk would change the way the cards were stacked against me.

On hindsight, it is funny how fear can force one into doing foolish things.

I knew I did not like my job and would have loved to do something different, but that was not the same thing as being sacked, was it?

I must have been sitting there for a while, lost in my thoughts, because when I heard a sudden noise behind me, the clock had struck nine.

'Hi, how are you guys doing today?' enquired Aman, taking the empty seat next to Subbu.

'Oh, we are doing great,' responded Subbu, sounding sarcastic as he always did when he was speaking to someone he did not like.

Aman was silenced, taken aback by Subbu's reaction.

Subbu's retort was followed by an uncomfortable silence when none of us spoke. It was as if we needed time to digest what Subbu had just said.

The message had been conveyed to Aman and he now sat surrounded by an uncomfortable silence. Aman was afraid to speak, lest he resurrected the devil within Subbu.

'You guys are still annoyed with what happened on Friday,' Aman said after what had been a long time.

Then he paused, but not for long fearing that if he waited, it would give Subbu another opportunity to take a dig at him. 'I had a chat with AM following the

1–1 meetings. AM praised you guys a lot. He told me that you had great potential, and all we needed to do was channel it in the right direction. AM really thinks highly of you two and probably that is the reason he wants to frighten you into taking things seriously.'

'Good morning,' said Parag, interrupting Aman as he walked into office; Bhau walked in close at his heels. Parag and Bhau had probably come in together. Bhau usually picked Parag up on his way to work.

'Let's go down for a bite,' suggested Parag giving us a surprised look. He was a little taken aback by the unwelcome guest we had at our desks.

I had been working on the module but knew that I could not progress further without help from Bhau. I was also happy that going down for a bite would provide us with an excuse to escape the sermon that Aman intended to bestow on us.

I went around the corner taking the longer route through the aisle between the lifts and the coffee machines, while the others stuck to the shorter route.

Rajni was not at her desk, she was still to get to office.

I ordered a sandwich for myself before walking over to the table where the others were sitting. We ate breakfast quietly with some small talk in between. None of us felt like talking. I was tempted to tell the others about my story but after looking at the presiding mood decided against it. I also did not want Aman to learn about my love towards writing.

Aman had joined us for breakfast and was trying to engage us in conversation, but with little success. 'Oh, I have to leave for a meeting,' he said before long, excusing himself. I wasn't sure if Aman really had a meeting to attend to or he was just trying to escape the hostility he was receiving from us.

'Must have remembered that he has to lick AM's seat clean before AM gets in,' said Subbu once Aman was out of hearing.

We all laughed but realized that there was something amiss.

We walked to the till to clear our bills, but were told that Aman had paid for all of us. I felt a little guilty for the way we had been behaving with Aman. I wondered why we had reacted the way we had. Aman was not a bad person. He was trying hard to get to know us but with little success. I felt that we should have been a little more considerate towards him. It was not right on our part to be so judgmental without having given him a fair chance.

'I think we are making a mistake. Aman seems to be a nice guy,' I said trying to give words to my thoughts.

'You know the problem with you, Anup, is that you trust people too easily,' said Subbu. 'I guess all this running around Rajni has done something to your head,' he finished, before rushing up the stairs in a huff.

'I don't like Aman either,' added Parag.

We did not speak about Aman anymore deciding to keep our thoughts to ourselves. I continued to wonder about what Subbu and Parag had said. I think I did agree with Subbu's observation that I always trusted people easily. Subbu had once told me that I had not seen enough of the world. His opinion was that the real world was outside the IT industry. The IT, according to Subbu, was all but an illusion where everyone was trying to outsmart each other, assuming that he or she was the smartest. He'd even said something to the effect: 'In India, IT is an illusion, where everyone wants more than what he has and everyone thinks, he or she deserves what they desire for.'

'But is that not true with the rest of the world,' I had retorted.

'Yes, it is probably true all over the world and not just in IT, but the difference in India is that the IT companies continue to feed and nurture the illusion,' Subbu replied before adding. 'It still works out cheaper for the companies, they don't mind it as long as the profits exist. And this will probably go on for a long time till either the employees tire from the wild goose chase realizing the futility of the whole process or the companies decide that the limits have been breached and they no longer wish to feed the illusion.'

'You are a fool Subbu,' I had answered unable to understand what he was driving at.

I am still not sure if I completely understand Subbu but I do agree with him that the world is outside the four walls of an IT company.

I spent the remainder of the morning, sitting in front of the computer screen and working on my modules. I had walked a few times to Bhau's desk to get clarifications on the component designs and to the coffee machine to fetch an occasional cup of tea, but other than that I had not moved from my desk.

~

I was at the coffee machine waiting for it to deliver my tea.

It was my fifth cup since morning and I had still not seen Rajni. Payal who occupied the cubicle next to Rajni's looked up at me and smiled. There was something about Payal's smile, which told me that it was not a friendly one.

The frustration of not finding Rajni at her seat was evident on my face. Payal must have noticed it and also observed the fact that I was frequenting the coffee machine. I was sure Payal would mention my transgression of Rajni's key rule of being discrete with our relationship in office, in one of her offhand conversations with Rajni.

From what I knew of Payal she would never miss an opportunity to berate me in front Rajni. I realized that I would have to check my urge of visiting the coffee machine.

'You drink a lot of tea,' I heard a voice from behind.

I was startled. I turned around to find Aman standing behind me.

'H-h- hi, sir,' I managed with a stutter.

'Oh, don't call me sir!'

'How is your work coming along?' he enquired, sounding rather amicable.

I was beginning to like Aman a little more each time we met. 'He is such a nice guy. I don't understand why Parag and Subbu hate him,' I wondered.

'I've got a lot of modules to code; it is quite complicated. I have been asking Bhau for help with certain issues, but I am sure I will finish the modules before they are due to be delivered,' I said, adding quickly, 'Bhau has designed the application so he understands the system better and knows a lot more about the modules.'

I hoped Aman would not get the impression that I could not complete my modules without help from Bhau. At the same time I did not want to sound like someone who was trying to take credit for something I had not done.

I knew there was little I could have done without Bhau's help, but a person has to fend for himself in the IT.

To survive in the IT jungle one has to constantly send out signals informing others about his or her presence. One has to ensure that his name appears on the symbolic list maintained by the higher management, if he wants to be promoted or even get a decent hike. You would not last a single day in IT, if you do not paint a positive picture of yourself to your colleagues or superiors. IT is a constant struggle where you can get killed if you lose your focus, even for a second. It is like driving on Indian roads where even the best of drivers can fail.

On Indian roads one has to constantly look out for mistakes made by others and take advantage from them; knowing how to drive does help, but only a little. If you are a careful driver who is averse to taking risks, you could end up spending hours in traffic congestions, while smarter drivers sneak through gaps left by the inept ones. If you are smart you can quickly learn to drive the Indian way, but if you are foolish or one of the heady nerds you'd be plain lucky to survive.

There were a few exceptions to the general rule, but only because they had godfathers inside the organization.

I quickly learnt that it was easy to drive through traffic congestion if you followed a bus or a big van. People ahead made way for the bigger vehicles fearing the clout thrown around by them and all one had to do to succeed was stay close at heels. You progress as the bigger vehicles move. This strategy compensated for my inability to learn quickly and take advantage from mistakes made by others. I was constantly making amends to my driving not because I wanted to win but because I did not want to get killed or get stuck in congestion.

Aman smiled before we started walking back to the desks.

'Anup, can you tell me a little more about the project and the organization? I wanted to ask you about this earlier, but did not find the opportune moment for it,' said Aman looking at me expectantly. 'It does not have to be immediately, give me a shout when you are free, and we can have a casual meeting round the corner,' Aman quickly added reading the uneasiness on my face.

We had reached the corner where we had to part ways to reach our desks.

It struck me that Aman had not bothered to collect a drink from the coffee machine. I assumed he had forgotten about it after running into me. It surely did not make sense for Aman to have walked all the way just to have a chat with me.

'I sure will,' I said, quickly heading back to my seat.

~

I probably would have accepted Aman's invitation right away, but for the fears lurking within me.

I realized that I would not be able to make progress with my modules until I could convince Bhau to assist me in understanding the component designs.

I was free until the time Bhau agreed to help me, but I knew, that in this industry even if you were free or, in other words, had nothing worthwhile to do, you had to act busy in order to avoid damaging your software rating.

I have always known that in the workplace every action, or rather every move you made, was rated. It was either your friends, your superiors or your subordinates who rated you. There always is a hidden spreadsheet on which the numbers move up or down based on your performance. This spreadsheet is evident with people like KK, but with others it is well hidden.

Visible or invisible, evident or hidden, the spreadsheet is always there.

Every morning when you wake up you hope that you lose only a few and gain a lot of points on your spreadsheet. It helps to remember that the numbers on your superior's spreadsheet matter more than the ones on your subordinates' or colleagues' spreadsheet.

People like AM have a poor rating on their subordinates' spreadsheets, but they always ensure that they get a high rating on their superiors' spreadsheets.

There are various techniques which one could employ to improve ratings in an organization. The simplest and the most preferred technique is sycophancy. There are various other techniques that one could use like CP (Credit Pinching), SA (Self Advertising) and MM (Malicious Mischief).

It would be foolish to deny the fact that working hard also helps, but if not used in combination with the other techniques, the chances of your ratings moving up significantly are pretty low.

Everyone that I have known in the IT industry uses CP in one way or the other. Some use CP knowingly while others do so, unaware.

I knew I was taking away a little of the credit that belonged to Bhau, but I had to do it in order to save my skin. I was using CP only to stay afloat. There were many who used CP to grow in the organization. AM was probably one of the most prolific user of this technique.

SA on the other hand is a technique that is very effective only when you know how to use it. SA is harder to master and tougher to implement but more rewarding than CP. SA not only ensures that people stand up and

take notice of your presence but it also makes sure that
your superiors remember you when it is time for hikes
and promotions. SA is most effective when used in
meetings, parties and big group discussions.

Last but not least, and probably the most dangerous
technique, is MM. It is a technique that should be only
used as a last resort when you have tried using both CP
and SA. While CP and SA are constructive and help you
gain points, MM is a destructive technique that is used to
reduce the points in someone else's spreadsheet. You only
used MM when you have failed with all the other
techniques, because if you are caught using MM it could
jeopardize your entire career.

AM was a prolific user of CP and a master at SA, a
deadly combination to have. The fact that AM was
intelligent and hard-working made him invincible. The
only way one could beat AM at his game was by using
MM but luckily for AM there was no one around who
knew how to use MM or was courageous enough to use
it.

I would later realize how wrong I was with my
inferences about MM.

8

JUST ANOTHER MANIC MONDAY—II

Every day at the workplace is a new dawn that brings with it new learnings. In an industry where everyone is fighting for a piece of the same pie, where no one accepts that they are not deserving enough for the size of pie they desire, it could be a nightmare if you are the one who is cutting the pieces.

You could dole out endless number of management jargons, you could rationalize your decisions on an illusory bell curve, you could feign helplessness because of higher gods in management or even quote the supreme soul in asking your subordinates to work without a lure for rewards, but never accept your failings as a manager or your inability in convincing your subordinates of their shortcomings.

If you are the one who is receiving the pie, it is always hard to be satisfied with the piece you have. The fact that you do not know the size of the piece of pie that has been handed to your colleagues makes it harder to digest.

You always end up with an indigestion assuming that your colleagues have received a bigger piece than what you think they deserve.

One might be tempted into thinking that the secrecy HR

shrouds around the hikes or promotions is a reason behind the troubles.

But the fact remains, if you are the one cutting the pieces, you can never make others feel happy about the size of the piece you hand out to them, and if you are one of the stakeholders in the pie, you will never be happy with the size you get . . . this is a simple rule of life and the biggest bane of IT.

~

'Hieeeeeeeeeee,' said an email popping out from the corner of my screen. I clicked on the box to open up the Outlook window.

'How are you doing?

'Not fair! You have not sent me a single email today. Is something wrong? Are you angry with me?

'I am sorry, baba, but Mama wanted me to do so many things and someone or the other was always around me. I just could not find time to call you after Saturday morning. My sister was always beside me wanting to share my happiness and of course the gifts. We had many visitors in the evening to wish me for the birthday.

'So, tell me, how was your weekend?' said the email from Rajni.

Rajni had no idea about what had transpired since Friday. I did not intend to discuss the situation with her.

I had not thought about Rajni till then, but now after reading her mail I felt upset about not being with her on her birthday and also about the fact that she hadn't called me after Saturday morning. The funny thing about our relationship was that she always had to tell me when I could rightly feel upset and jealous about something.

After having read her mail I felt vindicated about my

unhappy feelings and they grew as Rajni's support for them increased.

'Got a lot of work, need to finish coding before the weekend. So how did your birthday go? What did your parents give you?' I replied, not wanting to give away anything about my 1–1 with AM.

'You are lying to me, aren't you?' came back Rajni's reply.

'Nahi Baba, I am not lying. I seriously have a lot of work to catch up on!' I answered.

It was hard convincing Rajni once she had made her mind. Must have been something to with the bull-headed Taurus that she was, I thought.

'Want to meet today? We can go out to Nirula's for a quick bite,' said Rajni's next email.

She knew I could never refuse her! This was her way of comforting me and letting me know that she really cared.

~

We usually drove down to Nirula's once a month. It was the only time when we were alone. And this usually happened when Payal was on a holiday or when I was in a very bad mood, like today. Rajni thought that I was angry with her and was trying to placate me. I knew that today Rajni would answer to my every beck and call. I also had to give Rajni her gift, so, after a little persuasion, I agreed.

We decided that we would go out at 3.00 p.m. and be back in an hour's time. That would allow for Rajni to have lunch with Payal, Ashish and Nidhi before our meeting. It worked well with me because I would not have to provide Subbu with an explanation for skipping lunch.

~

Then I got back to coding, feeling a little guilty about having to leave my seat for an hour to meet Rajni. It was a battle that I was still fighting—a battle between the heart and the mind, when AM came to my desk.

'Hi, Anup! Hope you had a wonderful weekend. I have worked on a plan for us. I thought about it over the weekend and now it's ready. Could you please come with me to the meeting room and I can explain it to you?'

I locked my computer and collected my notebook before following AM to the meeting room. I could see Subbu smirking from the corner of my eye.

The next thirty minutes were spent in the meeting room with AM going through every detail of his master plan. AM, between praising himself, explained how he was going to constantly monitor me. I would have to provide AM with a detailed report every day for the next few weeks, following which AM would rethink his plan. If satisfied, he would move our updates to weekly or bi-weekly—I braced myself for tough times ahead.

He had carefully broken down every hour of my workday, thankfully leaving a few hours for lunch and other breaks. I thanked him for his thoughtfulness and wondered how I was ever going to meet his deadlines!

I was walking back to my desk completely engrossed in my thoughts when I ran into Aman who seemed to be in a great hurry.

'Got a meeting with AM to discuss how we are going

to deal with the new projects,' Aman said with a smile before rushing past me into the meeting room I had just vacated.

I dreaded the word 'projects' and more projects could only mean things much worse. Having started my career at a period where layoffs had been the norm, there was little choice about what was best for the industry.

Bhau still seemed wrapped up in his computer screen when I got back to my desk. I quickly unlocked my computer and tried to find out the best way to counter AM's task list.

Thankfully, I was pulled away from the complicated program by an invitation from Subbu to go for lunch. I was not feeling hungry at the moment; all the fuss AM had created at the meeting had tied my stomach in knots. I refused Subbu's invitation and went back to coding my module. I realized, I had lot of work to do if I was going to go out with Rajni and still meet AM's deadlines.

I watched as Subbu, Parag and Bhau left for lunch.

I felt a pang of guilt run through me. I wasn't even sure if the guilt was justified, but there was little time to think along those lines.

I was back to my computer coding 0s and 1s.

Time flew faster than ever before, and soon it was 3.00 p.m.

I received an email from Rajni 'I am leaving now, come to the car after five minutes.'

I counted exactly 300 seconds before leaving my desk and I walked out without sparing a glance for the others. Rajni was waiting near the car for me. She was wearing a white shirt with black stripes and black trousers. The colour of her shirt made her look even fairer. I quickly got into the car and opened the door for her.

We drove out of the car park into the highway.

Rajni seemed very excited; she was rather too chirpy for the time of the day. She had a lot of stories to tell me. I sat there listening but not responding to anything she said. She did enquire a few times if everything was fine, but I had just nodded without adding any words.

I was still thinking about AM's task list and the meeting and was feeling bad about having left my desk when I needed to work on the modules. I thought I was failing myself in my determination to change, to display my potential.

I swerved the car suddenly realizing that engrossed in my thoughts I was about to over shoot the exit towards the little-used old road.

This branch of Nirula's that we were heading towards was located on the old road that had made way for the new national highway, and hence had very few connoisseurs. The only reason this branch had been left open was probably for the likes of Rajni and me.

Rajni was still on a high note when we entered Nirula's.

I ordered her a sundae and myself a cup of tea before joining her at the corner table near the window. The corner seat was our favourite as it was farthest from the serving counter and allowed us to talk to our hearts' content without anyone overhearing us.

I watched Rajni's hair bounce around her face as she went about telling me everything that had happened since last Thursday, about her birthday and the weekend. She had just completed telling me about the visit from her grandparents, when our order arrived.

Once the waiter had left, Rajni complained about how

full her stomach was after the lunch but soon started eating the ice cream hungrily. I knew about Rajni's weakness for ice cream and chocolates. I slowly sipped my tea while I watched her eat her ice cream. The ice cream left a line on Rajni's lips. I smiled at her, trying to take in the fact that the beautiful girl sitting across me at the table was mine.

I wished I could wipe the line away from Rajni's face.

'Come on, take a bite. It is wonderful!' she offered.

'No, I am drinking tea,' I replied, smiling back at her.

I was slowly forgetting my nightmare at office. The only thought in my mind was about how beautiful Rajni looked then. I wished I could freeze this moment.

'Oh, come on, have a bite. Nothing will happen!' she begged, taking a spoonful and bringing it close to my mouth.

I knew better than to refuse Rajni. She looked pretty adamant. I took a bite thinking about how things had changed. The first time I had seen Rajni, she and Payal were having an argument. Rajni had been furious that Payal had eaten from her plate.

'I don't eat *jhoota*!' Rajni had fumed.

I felt wonderful! AM was the last thing on my mind.

'You know they are planning on making a news magazine for the company. My manager has asked me to be a part of the editorial panel. I am really excited! There is so much to do. I am also working with Rajeev and Sandeep on the training plan for the new joinees.'

She puckered her nose when the ice-cream accidentally touched it, she looked very cute.

I guessed that her project was probably going through some kind of slump at the moment.

IT companies have developed a way of keeping active minds busy when there is little else to do in terms of projects, or, in other words, when the employees are on the bench. There are various initiatives that the companies have started in order to keep the employees occupied. One of them is publishing an in-house magazine. How else could one explain the need for a magazine? We were a software company after all!

As a result of such initiatives, we were now left with 'project tasks'—tasks for which one could bill a client and 'filler' tasks that had been started with the intention of keeping employees on bench occupied.

I wondered who came up with all these ideas because once the expectations had set in you could never let go of the filler tasks completely. They stayed even after the project work had picked up.

So at the end of the day, an employee was left to complete his project tasks along with the fillers. Not only this, the filler tasks even found a way into the objectives alongside the project tasks. Only a superhuman could manage to complete his work and have enough time left to spend on such initiatives.

I did not give words to my thoughts and continued listening to Rajni. She soon finished the ice cream and we walked back to the car. When I started the car and shifted to first gear I felt a cold touch on my hand. I looked down and my whole body tingled with excitement.

Rajni had placed her hand over mine—her hand was still cold from the ice cream.

I moved the car slowly out of the parking lot.

'Will you teach me how to drive?' she asked seductively.

'Sure I will, dear, once we are married,' I replied as I pulled the car onto the main road.

'Can you pull over for a while?' she asked, sounding far

away. My heart started beating loudly. What did Rajni have in mind? I felt my thoughts deserting me as my mind went numb, a warm sensation rose through my body.

'No, no. Park behind the tree. That way no one can see us,' she said as I pulled to the corner.

I was completely befuddled, not knowing what to do, I followed her instructions. Rajni's hold on my hand grew firmer.

'I love you a lot, Anup,' she said before tilting her head away from me towards the opposite window.

Rajni was blushing and did not want me notice it.

I moved closer and pulled her face towards me. I could feel the waft of Rajni's breath hit me. I was surrounded by a sweet smell. The magic continued as I pulled Rajni's face closer to mine.

'Trrrrrrrrrrrrrrrrrrrring,' Rajni's phone suddenly started ringing.

'Hello,' said Rajni, picking up the phone. She spoke into the phone for a while before placing it back on the dashboard.

The moment had passed!

We looked at each other before quickly turning away, afraid to acknowledge what had just passed between us.

'Love you too,' I said trying to disperse the sudden uneasiness that the call had left between us, before asking what the phone call was about.

'Oh, I had completely forgotten about the meeting we are having this afternoon. They are celebrating Holi at the office. We are planning to decorate the whole office. How exciting naaaa?' said Rajni.

Rajni was transformed back to her office self. I smiled

ruefully before starting the car and driving back to a place I could now refer to as HELL.

~

In the parking lot I walked to the rear of the car and opened the hatch. I pulled out the Shoppers Stop bag, and handed it over to Rajni. She opened the bag and pulled the blue shirt out and examined it for a while. I could make out that she had liked it.

'It is beautiful Anup! I asked you not to get me any gifts.' She was trying to sound angry but I knew she didn't mean it.

'Keep it with you, and I will pick it up later. I can't walk into office with the bag. Imagine what Payal and the others will think about my walking in with a shopping bag. I will come to get it when I leave in the evening,' she said before rushing to the lift.

I locked the car and walked towards the stairs.

~

Subbu, Parag and Bhau were all seated in Bhau's cubicle. They were sipping tea, engrossed in a serious discussion.

'What's wrong?' I asked them as I walked towards the group.

'Welcome back,' said Subbu, sounding like his sarcastic self.

Bhau looked up ruefully. I looked towards Parag. He seemed to be the sanest of the lot.

'AM just came over and told us that the client has sent in new timelines. We have to deliver the code in half the time. AM mentioned that this was make or break for the organization. These are hard times for the company because of the recession and talks about takeover. AM thinks that this is the only way of keeping the costs under control,' said Parag. Then he added, 'Of course, AM followed it up with his management jargon and a wonderful speech on how he thought we delivered much less than the industry average.'

I stared at the group for a while before walking back to my machine and logging on. There was no way I was going to meet my existing deadlines. If what the group said was true, then I would probably have to double my pace of work.

9

THE BIRTHDAY PARTY

It had been three days since my meeting with AM. I was sitting at my desk working hard on the module. I had not moved from my seat for nearly an hour. I envisaged it was going to be another busy day at work. We had less than a month to meet the deadlines the client had set.

AM had all but forgotten about his daily update meeting with me. The meetings and status checks that the client insisted on was probably taking up most of his time. Any leftover time was taken up by KK and his spreadsheets. I, at times, pitied AM. Unlike KK before him, AM involved himself in the day-to-day trudge of project work. He not only reviewed our modules but also took on additional responsibility of coding the harder modules along with Bhau.

Aman had come up to our desks and offered to help with the codes, but there seemed to be many other things pulling him away. So it seemed like he was watching us from the sidelines. I sometimes got the feeling that Aman was shying away from the tasks, feigning lack of system knowledge or acting busy in trying to understand his new responsibilities. It looked like he did not want to be involved in this situation.

Subbu thought Aman was play-acting and didn't really intend to be of any help. Parag had no views about Aman, his IITian brain was busy finding ways to reduce the workload. If only Parag had spent more time on the work at hand instead of finding nonexistent solutions, we would be in much better shape. I probably deserved a bigger share of the blame, but then who was counting?

~

On Thursday, three days after our tryst at Nirula's, Rajni finally managed to find some free time from her hectic schedule.

It was the fourth day on the trot where Rajni and her team had done little to add to the company's sagging revenues. Rajni's and her team were on the bench, working hard on the training plan, in-house magazine, Holi celebrations and a few other so-called important tasks.

'Payal and Ashish are insisting on a party. Can we go today, pleaseeeeee? You have been refusing since Monday and now it is Thursday. They think I do not want to take them out,' popped the email from Rajni, drawing me away from the module that I had been working on.

Rajni had been postponing her birthday treat because of her creative activities in the office rather than my hectic schedule. But she had conveniently put me in the position of the scapegoat. For her everything had to be rationalized as someone else's fault. And here I was ready to be in the line of fire! I wasn't foolish enough to share my views with her, but I seethed underneath. The additional hours at work were taking their toll; I was turning into a grumpy old man.

Stress can do funny things to people. Stress can even make you think that everyone around is scheming against you. It was like I was fighting the world along with the modules and component designs.

There were many defects in my first module that I was yet to fix. AM had reviewed my module and sent me a list of about fifty comments. I had cursed AM, thinking how picky he was about the code. One of AM's comments had been around the extra blank lines I had inserted between paragraphs in the modules. I had forgotten to delete them in a hurry. AM had also mentioned that the blank lines would end up taking more space on the disk and hence should be deleted. Subbu and I had laughed at the comment and also a few others from AM. We conveniently ignored AM's more relevant comments around program logic and when we mentioned the irrelevant comments to Bhau he had clenched his teeth in frustration.

~

Subbu agreed to let me attend Rajni's birthday party after putting up a huge fuss. I don't remember why I had even bothered asking Subbu for permission or tried to convince him about it. I probably did it partly to absolve myself of guilt and partly to ensure that there was someone who would help me with the modules if I could not meet the deadlines AM had set.

~

It was noon, I stood leaning against the front door of my car, outside the office gates, waiting for Rajni and her troupe. I had parked the car under a small tree, a little away from the office gates.

Rajni had wanted me to get the car outside in order to save everyone the ordeal of walking down to the basement car park. There I stood, leaning against the car, thinking about Rajni and our previous meeting. I felt a warmth engulf me when I recollected how close Rajni and I had been to kissing each other. The sun was overhead, waiting, before it started to make it's descent towards the west. There was little to protect me from it other than the sparse shade of a tree. I felt the first beads of sweat trickle down my forehead. The heat was not the usual unbearable kind that is common during the summers. It was March, the winter had just receded and the summer was still a month away. The occasional wind helped ease the temperatures.

I was getting tired of waiting and decided to switch on the music system. As I turned around and opened the front door, I spotted Ashish walking towards the car. I forgot the music and shut the door assuming that the others were close at heel.

Inside, I felt a sudden twinge of jealousy hit me as I watched Ashish walk towards the car. I hated Ashish for his closeness to Rajni.

Ashish had joined our organization a year back, straight from college. In certain ways he was still a kid, yet to put behind his college days. He thought the company as an extension of his classes at college. As a result, he was living the dream that most of us had shared during our college days—of making it big in life. It would only be a few more months before he would realize that things in the IT world were very different from his dreams.

I spotted Nidhi and Payal walking out of the gate a few

seconds later . . . They had been unable to keep up with Ashish's pace because of the heels on their shoes that made walking much tougher.

I sometimes wondered why girls endured the heels when apart from making them a few inches taller there was no other purpose they served!

I was hoping Rajni would take the front seat. I did not want Ashish to sit with me. I was always looking for these small signs from Rajni. I considered them a personal victory because they proved to the world that Rajni was mine. I sometimes silently prayed for them. It was these small signs which provided me with comfort as I tried to hide our relationship from the world.

It was little things that Rajni did, like sitting next to me during lunch, taking the front seat of the car when we went out as a group, saving sweets or other eatables for me, finding reasons to include me in outings with her friends, which were the signs that I cherished.

Rajni, I think, never noticed or did what she did intentionally. Rajni probably would have behaved the same way for any other friend of hers.

I, unknown to Rajni, continued to build my expectations and derive pleasure when things went my way.

It usually started out with a small thought like the one about Rajni taking the front seat. Then these thoughts kept tossing in my mind and soon became desires and then I started longing for them to happen. I wished that my desires would come true and prayed for them. I was happy when things turned out the way I had thought them out and wished for, but when they did not I could become very annoyed or cranky.

Rajni never seemed to understand why I behaved the

way I did during such times. I never thought it important to explain to her, because I was both afraid that I might sound childish and I assumed that things should have been obvious to her in the first place.

The times when things did not turn out the way I wanted them to were always hard on our relationship. There was a small void between us that seemed to get bigger every time something like that happened. I tried hard to fight my sudden urges but always lost my battle in the end. No matter how hard I tried convincing myself that these small actions of Rajni were inconsequential, I always ended up thinking otherwise.

I knew it would be impossible for Rajni to take the seat next to me, when Payal was with us. I hated Payal even more for it. I knew Rajni would take the rear seat alongside Payal, leaving the front seat for either Ashish or Nidhi, but that did little to relieve me of my desire. I knew I was going to be cranky during the drive to the restaurant but there was little I could do to avoid it. I was helpless and resigned to my fate.

I could now see the outline of Nidhi's and Payal's faces clearly. Nidhi noticed me watching them and smiled. I smiled back at her. The previous thoughts apart, I liked Nidhi the most amongst Rajni's friends.

Nidhi looked charming as always. Her shoulder length hair formed a protective shield around her ears. Nidhi's hair unlike Rajni's, were straight, devoid of all the curls that made Rajni's hair seem so unruly and hard to manage. They weren't jet black like Rajni's but were of a lighter shade making them look soft and elegant.

Nidhi was almost as tall as Rajni, but her thin frame made her look taller. It got accentuated by the way she carried herself. She had a long face with firm jawbones that gave her a beautiful sculpted look. Her features were very sharp and her dusky complexion only added to the effect she had on people. She was always smiling. It was easy to instantly start liking Nidhi.

I had noticed Nidhi for the first time at a friend's wedding, the same wedding where Rajni had made me jealous because of the attention that the photographer was bestowing on her. Nidhi looked completely transformed that night. It was the make-up and the surroundings that had brought about the change. Rajni had looked beautiful that night but Nidhi made your heart long for her. If Rajni was a beautiful doll, Nidhi looked like a girl from your dream who you never thought you would meet.

Every time I noticed Nidhi smile I felt my heart wavering between my love for Rajni and desire for Nidhi.

At the wedding, for the first time since I had expressed my love for Rajni, I had felt my heart vacillating. It was the first time I felt myself questioning the feelings that my heart harboured for Rajni. I had frequently stolen glances at Nidhi between admiring the way Rajni looked that night.

It was the jealously that I felt because of the photographer and the hundreds of compliments that Rajni had received from others that had helped me stay firm.

My feeling was that Rajni had also probably read my thoughts that night; she had probably noticed me stealing glances at Nidhi because from then on, she had always seemed annoyed when I mentioned Nidhi's name in our conversations. She fought hard to hide her discomfort when she saw me with Nidhi.

I was banking on this weakness when I wished for her to sit next to me in the car.

Payal was also accompanying us that evening. She was beautiful, but came across as dumb and arrogant. If I did not have to go through the constant struggle she posed for me in order to save my relationship with Rajni, I would have thought of Payal as a pretty girl next door. I think most of my views about Payal were because of her reluctance to accept the relationship I shared with Rajni.

I thought of Payal as a garrulous person. She reminded me of my mother's friends who had made berating others the sole purpose of their lives, deriving pleasure from making others' lives miserable.

I wondered how anyone could live with the likes of Payal and Ashish. They had the tendency to get under your skin, but, unlike AM, they were not dangerous.

Rajni had once told me how Payal had confided to her about me.

'I think you should stay away from Anup,' Payal had said before adding. 'He seems to be drooling all over you. I think there is something wrong with him,' she had added.

I had laughed and said to Rajni, 'It's your fault, since you have yet to tell your friends about our relationship.'

I still remember the expression Rajni had on her face when she had told me that story. I had foolishly believed that there was no one Rajni hated more in her life than Payal. And was even more surprised to find Rajni and Payal engrossed deep in conversation the next day in office. They were back to being the inseparable pair that they always were!

'Girls,' I had thought.

～

'Hi, Anup,' said Nidhi as they neared the car. Nidhi was wearing a white salwar kameez that highlighted her features and complexion in a very likeable way.

'Hi,' I replied before adding, 'where is Rajni?'

'Oh, she had some urgent work in the training room. She'll be joining us soon,' replied Ashish.

I looked at Ashish accusingly but he did not seem to have noticed me.

Ashish and Payal had started a conversation among themselves ignoring me and Nidhi completely.

There was an uncomfortable silence between me and Nidhi as we waited for Rajni.

The relationship between Payal and me had never been good enough to allow for conversation beyond pleasantries. I hated Ashish and did not want to talk to him.

I allowed Payal and Ashish to continue with what looked like a childish banter as they surrounded themselves with giggles. I did not want to speak to Nidhi either, fearing that Payal would use it as bait against me with Rajni.

So while Ashish and Payal giggled at their childish pranks, I and Nidhi looked away trying to seem engrossed in our thoughts.

~

Rajni had taken to Ashish from his first day in her team. I like to think that Ashish probably reminded Rajni of a younger brother she always desired for but never had.

Ashish on the other hand had taken to Rajni like an abandoned puppy. He had not only shared all his intimate secrets with Rajni but also confided in her about his innermost thoughts. He consulted her about every important decision that he had to make. It was not unusual to find both Rajni and Ashish sitting in the cafeteria or on their desks talking for hours on end.

Rajni being what she was had yet to tell Ashish about our relationship.

Ashish was always by Rajni's side inside the office. The fact that they were assigned to the same project and Rajni was Ashish's mentor made things worse.

When I wanted to meet Rajni alone, Ashish at times proved to be a bigger hindrance than Payal. Things had reached a stage where Rajni insisted on having lunch with Ashish because he would go without lunch if Rajni would forget to invite him! This was partly because Rajni usually brought food from home for Ashish.

At times I would feel jealous and at other times dismiss the developments with a smile. Rajni and I were passing thorough the hardest test that our relationship had ever been put through.

Ashish had grown very protective about Rajni and probably would have done anything to have her for himself. Ashish's intentions did not seem very noble then. He had once come down to my desk trying to build ill will between me and Rajni. I had heard him out before telling him off . . . The next day I had met Rajni and her group over coffee and Ashish had behaved like nothing had passed between us.

Later that week I had confided in Rajni but she had laughed it off quoting Ashish's immaturity as the reason for it. It had made me furious but I just could not seem to reason with Rajni and win her sympathy. I was finally forced to accept Rajni's explanation that Ashish was young and behaved so because he did not want to lose the support he had found in Rajni.

I had accepted Rajni's explanation not because I was convinced but because I did not want to argue with her. I loved her a lot.

I had tried again in a few weeks time, when things between Ashish and Rajni became unbearable.

'Rajni, I don't like you mixing with Ashish! I don't like it when you and Ashish sit for hours and talk in the office. I don't like him. He is taking advantage of you.'

Rajni had initially laughed it off and then gone silent. She had stood still for a while, like the calm before the storm.

'Anup, you are behaving like a kid! Ashish is three years younger to me,' she had said before leaving in a huff.

I had tried to explain but failed miserably and ended up feeling guilty about the whole scene. I thought I was behaving just like the possessive boyfriend from the movies.

The incident, though, had done little to reduce my ill will towards Ashish.

The worst part of the whole affair was that Ashish never seemed to understand how I felt. I had once taken him aside and explained to him in the best possible way that Rajni was my girl. All that it had done was make Ashish act in a way that annoyed me even more.

Over the past months, Rajni and I had agreed never to discuss Ashish because we were never able to get our point across to each other.

~

Rajni arrived, saving all of us from burning to ashes. The noon sun added to the uncomfortably long silence between Nidhi and me was killing.

'Let's go,' said Rajni, getting into the back seat.

Ashish, just to annoy me, got into the back seat next to Rajni; Payal joined them.

I clenched my teeth and started the car. Nidhi took the front seat next to me.

Ashish was whispering something into Rajni's ears and then he repeated the same to Payal. The three broke into laughter, making Nidhi and me feel even more uncomfortable than before.

We finally arrived at the restaurant. Ashish stuck by Rajni's side like a moth attracted to light.

Nidhi and I walked towards the counter trying to decide the menu. Payal, Rajni and Ashish, still engrossed in their conversation, walked to the closest empty table.

I was furious with Rajni. Rajni sitting in the rear seat had annoyed me but her actions now were driving me mad. She seemed so engrossed in the conversation with Ashish and Payal that she had completely forgotten me and Nidhi. I was tempted to do something foolish to win my Rajni back. I asked Nidhi to queue up before walking to the table where the others were sitting in order to give their preferences for lunch. Nidhi and I ordered for the whole group before joining the other three at the table.

I fought hard to control my anger. It took a while before our token numbers were called for. Ashish and Nidhi helped me in collecting the order.

Once the orders had arrived and everyone was busy relishing what they had ordered, I excused myself to visit the restroom. I washed my face and pushed back the tears of frustration before returning to the table.

Ashish had taken the seat next to Rajni.

I took the corner seat opposite to where Rajni had been sitting a while ago and started eating quietly, making little conversation.

Others were enjoying themselves, while I imagined how I would love to strangle Ashish. I wished I could have brought Subbu and the others along.

I slowly moved my leg under the table to touch Rajni's feet. Rajni looked up startled and stared at me when our feet touched. I pulled my leg back wondering why she was behaving in this way. Then as we neared the end of our lunch, I signalled the waiter to bring the cake that I had ordered on the way back from the restroom. Rajni was delighted, but the cake seemed to have annoyed Payal. The cake had fortified Payal's belief about me.

I watched as Rajni cut the cake. Payal picked up a piece and plastered it on Rajni's face. Nidhi did the same. Everyone was looking at our table by now. I sat in the corner watching the proceedings like the others in the restaurant around us. Rajni was very happy, she was too engrossed in the fun to notice me.

Ashish brought some tissues from the counter. He even helped Rajni wipe the cake pieces stuck to her face.

I stood up in frustration and walked to the counter to pay for the cake.

~

The return journey was much better because everyone was quiet. They had all realized how furious I was. I was sure each one of them had their own interpretation of my reaction.

I dropped the others near the office gate before driving down to the parking to park my car and returning to my desk.

I opened the component design and tried to pull my thoughts away from the forgettable party.

A few minutes later, there was an email from Rajni. 'Thank you for the wonderful party! But you could have at least smiled,' it had read.

There was little I could say or do to change things so I went back to my component design without bothering to reply to Rajni's mail.

~

The work at hand helped me keep my mind away from all the other thoughts. Rajni and I went into a week-long feud before we gave up the battle and got back together.

10

BHAU

The components had to be shipped out this evening, and I still had five modules to complete. I looked around sheepishly, hoping that I could find someone and convince him to help me complete my tasks before the deadline.

There was no sign of Bhau. Parag and Subbu were also missing from their seats.

I struggled to complete the work as the deadline drew closer.

Bleary-eyed I struggled to understand what the component design wanted from the modules I was coding. Then, in desperation, I stood up again, hoping to catch a glimpse of Bhau, but he was still missing from his seat.

I looked around at the empty office before getting back to my computer screen. 'Where has everyone disappeared?' I was still stuck in a dilemma, trying hard to find a solution to my troubles when my desk phone suddenly started ringing. The ring seemed to echo through the empty office. I shuddered before picking the receiver up.

It was AM at the other end. He wanted me to join him in the meeting room.

I had still to start work on four modules and there was no way

I was going to finish them before the deadline. I braced myself for what was to come. Realizing that this meeting could be my last, I slowly walked to the meeting room, fearing the worst. Once there, I·sat myself on a chair close to the exit door. I stared at the floor, not having enough courage to look up at the faces around me.

I wasn't sure if Bhau, Subbu and Parag were in the meeting room, but it hardly mattered any more. No one could save me, it was too late even for prayers.

I needed a miracle to bail me out.

I had been under observation for the last few weeks, and this mishap probably signalled the end of my career.

'Anup,' I heard AM's voice. He seemed to be shouting and his voice seemed to come from a distance, 'I am sorry, but even after having provided you with innumerable opportunities to improve and after having given you all the assistance I could, I am yet to find any signs of improvement. You have closed all the doors and there is only one option that I have,' said AM.

I had a sense of foreboding about what was coming next. My head was bursting and the pain in my throat was hurting unbearably . . . I was grasping for breath· . . . I felt the walls collapsing around me . . .

'Anup, Anup, wake up!' I heard a voice calling me from far away. I felt a tug on my shoulder and suddenly sat up on my bed. Dad was standing beside me. I was sweating profusely, still a little incoherent after the nightmare.

'Anup, Subbu is on the phone. He wants to talk to you urgently,' said Dad as he pushed the mobile towards me.

'Hello,' I said groggily as Dad stood by my side watching intently, trying to understand what the problem was.

I faintly heard Subbu's voice from other end. 'Anup, Bhau has had an accident. He is in the ICU at Safdarjung,' Subbu managed before the line got disconnected.

I looked up, dazed with what I had just heard. Dad gave me a worried glance.

'Dad, Bhau has had an accident and is in ICU at Safdarjung Hospital,' I managed to repeat before trying to recollect my thoughts.

~

Dad and I dressed quickly while Mom scurried around the house trying to digest the news that she had just heard. She was trying hard to be of help but was only making matters worse with her hysterical questioning on what had happened to Bhau.

Dad refused to let her come with us. He thought that it was best for someone to stay back in case something was needed from the house. We walked out promising to call with all the details as soon as we got there.

~

It was about two in the morning. Thankfully, the roads were empty. I drove as fast as I could, negotiating the turns as best our car would allow and reached Safdarjung hospital twenty minutes later.

A dishevelled Parag sat on a chair while Subbu was pacing around helplessly.

~

Bhau hailed from a small town in Maharashtra where his father was a schoolteacher who had retired a few years back. Being the youngest of the four children and the only male child he was much adored by his parents and family. With the venerated position that Bhau held also came extraordinary responsibility. His family was totally dependent on him for all their financial needs. Combined with this was the additional responsibility of getting his sisters married.

Burdened by the extra responsibilities on his shoulders, Bhau had matured faster than any of us. He was proof that maturity can come with life's experiences and not just from years you have spent living. Bhau's age could not be measured in years that he had left behind.

Bhau had been brought up by a teacher, which was one of the reasons why he had the pillars of his life firmly etched. He never did anything that he considered unethical or unfair. When the entire office scavenged for bills during the final months of the tax year, Bhau refrained from making any false claims.

Even if he probably deserved the tax money more than any of us, he was the only person who paid all his taxes without fail.

I had heard from one of Bhau's classmates back at college that during his final year of engineering he had refused to write his exam because he had spotted the exam supervisor aiding another student in cheating. Bhau had walked into principal's office, leaving his exam papers unfinished, demanding justice.

The examiner had been later sacked but Bhau had stood his ground demanding action against the student even though the student Bhau had complained against, was the son of a high-placed official which made matters worse.

In the end Bhau had won his battle but not before having to rewrite his exams next year. He had lost a year fighting for justice and had yet failed to see reason.

Bhau had failed to understand that there were things in life that you needed to close your eyes to.

Bhau had failed to understand that there was nothing to gain by fighting battles for others or fighting a losing battle.

Bhau had failed to see light and hence had always paid the price.

And thus, Bhau was the only man who relentlessly fought our battles for us. For him, his ethics had been his greatest achievement in life.

For us he was the 'complete man'.

~

We had been working late for the last few weeks in order to meet the project deadlines. It was around midnight when I had reached home. Mom had been annoyed and was unable to understand what had kept me at work that long.

I ate my dinner silently before going to bed. I was too drained mentally to do anything else.

~

The smell of medicines assailed me as I stood next to Subbu who was sitting on the bench outside the ICU. I hoped that all this was nothing more than a bad dream.

I watched the frantic activity going on around us. There were people constantly walking in and out of the door to the emergency ward.

There were people in all kinds of state: crying, praying, people who had gone numb from the pain and also people who were slowly dying.

I stood there watching them realizing that on the other side of the wall people were battling for their lives, some of whom might not see the light of day.

Bhau could be one of those ill-fated ones.

I bit my lips as I watched an old woman sitting across me wiping her tears while praying in between sobs. I later learnt she had lost her husband to drinking a week ago and was now back in the hospital because her son had been caught in a feud.

Parag had walked out for a smoke. He needed fresh air to forget the pain that surrounded us.

Hospitals always made me feel sick in my stomach. An unknown fear seems to grip me every time I walk into one.

I spotted Dad walking back after having spoken to the doctor. The doctor had assured him that Bhau was now out of danger and there was nothing to worry about, they had done a CT scan and had found no damage to the brain. We sighed with relief.

~

Dad was getting ready to leave when Parag walked in along with a police officer. Since it was an accident case, the doctor had insisted on registering a police case before he could start treating Bhau. The police officer was here for the proceeding investigation.

'What is wrong?' enquired Dad, walking towards them.

'Uncle, the police say they will have to charge Bhau for drunken driving,' replied Parag.

Dad requested the police officer to hold until the morning when we would all be in a better shape to help him in his investigation.

It was an hour before the officer left, satisfied with what he had learnt. Dad left us promising to bring something to eat in the morning.

There was not much left for us to do except drinking tea from the attached cafeteria and to be available when the doctor or the nurse wanted us.

～

We called up Bhau's family in the morning and informed them about the accident. To keep them from panicking we told them that there was nothing serious and that things were under control. They were, naturally, worried and wanted to know if they needed to rush to Delhi. We reassured them and asked them to take time wrapping things up before coming. There really was no point in worrying them since Bhau was now out of danger and on his way to recovery. The only reason we wanted Bhau's dad to come over was to take care of him in our absence, since we would have to go to office sooner or later.

～

However, morning brought along a few more worries and troubles.

I called up office and informed AM that we would not be able to come in that day because of the accident. AM reluctantly agreed but reminded me that there was lot of work to be done at office. He also stressed on the fact that once back we might need to stay back in office to catch up on lost time.

'Is this project more important than a person's life?' I had blurted out seething in anger as I narrated the conversation with AM to Subbu and Parag. It was really amazing for me that people could be so callous at times like these.

Soon Mom and Dad arrived with breakfast. Mom insisted that two of us should go home and get some sleep while she stayed back with Bhau. Parag and I dropped Dad at his office before driving home for some much needed sleep. Subbu and Mom waited at the hospital.

When we returned that afternoon, Bhau had been shifted to a private ward. Subbu was sleeping on the spare bed while Mom watched the TV in silent mode.

We had brought along some change for Subbu.

Parag and I took turns at the hospital that night.

~

Bhau's dad had called up twice during the day wanting to talk to his son. We were no longer able to come up with convincing excuses. As a result the very next morning, Bhau's dad, fearing the worst, flew in. Parag and I went to the airport to receive him. He looked very old. Much older than the photos Bhau had shown us of him. It was probably the news of his son's accident that had made him age overnight. He did not stop asking us questions till we reached the hospital.

~

It had been two days since we had gone to office. When we did, we were rushed into the meeting room for a quick discussion with AM.

'The first batch of code has to be delivered in two weeks' time,' he said gravely. 'At this rate, however, there is no way we are going to meet the deadlines. There has been a substantial loss of time and you will need to stay back after office hours to catch up on the work,' he added before letting us leave the meeting room. Aman had also been present at the meeting. He sat silently watching the proceedings without commenting on anything. When he met us after the meeting, he promised to help us with the pending tasks.

That was the last I saw of Aman in office that day. It was most likely that he had been pulled away for some other important tasks.

AM had taken Bhau's desk and was now working on both his own modules and Bhau's. I wondered how AM wished to finish so much work so quickly.

~

That evening when we finished our day's work before heading to the hospital, AM was still toiling away at Bhau's desk.

~

At the hospital, Bhau's father sat motionless on the bedside, worried sick about his only son. He was still trying to come to terms with the tragedy, wondering where he had gone wrong to have deserved this fate for his son.

Bhau had begun to talk a little since morning, but his speech was slurred. Bandages covered his head and most of his face. He had lost a lot of blood and two bottles of drip were constantly running to replenish his lost fluids. He had also fractured two of the bones in his ribcage from the impact with the car. The doctor had informed us that there were no signs of slipped disc yet but we would have to wait till Bhau had recovered for confirmation. His right leg was in a cast and there were bandages around his elbows and wrists. Sadly, Bhau had lost his front teeth and the doctor had said that it would be months before the injuries on his face completely healed. Some of the scars, he'd said, would remain for life.

Suddenly, the bedside phone rang.

Subbu answered it, speaking for a while before placing back the receiver. 'It is KK. He and Aman are waiting at the reception.'

Subbu returned a few minutes later with KK and Aman in tow.

'How is Chetan now?' enquired KK as they walked in.

It was a little odd to see KK without his spreadsheets.

Later, both KK and Aman sat at Bhau's bedside talking to his father and comforting him. Aman even offered to spend the night at the hospital, but we gently refused, reassuring him that we had things in control.

As Aman and KK got ready leave Bhau's father suddenly broke down holding on to KK's hand.

'The police were here this morning,' he said. 'They want to file a case against Chetan. The owner of the car Chetan hit is insisting on filing a case.'

Bhau's dad blamed himself for the accident that had befallen on his son. He was sure that they had done something wrong in order to anger the gods into willing such a misfortune on his son.

He feared for the future of his son. He fretted over the thought that he was yet to get his daughters married. Where would he get the resources needed to get them married from? How would they get by if Bhau did not recover completely. These thoughts troubled him endlessly as he spent the entire morning tending to his only son. His thoughts were replaced by concern when Bhau shrieked with agony as the effect of the painkillers weakened. Soon, he was filled with remorse when Bhau winced of pain at the injections. The pain turned into misery when Bhau could not eat food because of his facial injuries.

~

Unable to continue working on the computer, I had finally logged off at around 11.00 p.m. that night. I wished Bhau and Subbu goodnight before walking down to the parking lot. Parag had not been feeling well and had left an hour earlier. Bhau had continued to work without a break trying to make the deadline. He was fighting against time trying to finish the work single-handedly.

After I left, Subbu managed to convince Bhau to leave around midnight. Then they had stopped on the way home at Shiva's to grab a bite. Shiva's was probably the only restaurant around that stayed open late into the night. Once inside, they'd been enticed by the liquor store next door. One drink led to another and before long, both of them were dead drunk.

This, however, was not the first time this had happened. Subbu and Bhau stayed close to office and hence the thought of having to drive in an inebriated state did not trouble them. And, they had done something similar a number of times before.

When they had paid their bills, they walked unsteadily towards the bike. However, quite uncharacteristically, Bhau had handed Subbu the keys to the bike when they walked out of Shiva's.

Subbu was surprised at Bhau's sudden change of mind but had not read much into it. He started the bike offering to drop off Bhau before heading to his own flat. But Bhau had refused Subbu's offer vehemently. So Subbu had given up trying to convince him and drove to his flat first.

He had watched Bhau drive into the night as he himself tottered into his flat.

It was an hour later, when Subbu had been woken up by a phone call from someone at the hospital, informing him that Bhau was at the Safdarjung Hospital.

~

What we later learnt about the accident was that Bhau had driven into the wrong side of the highway, wanting to take the shorter route home. We usually used the wrong side because it did away with the necessity of having to drive a mile before finding the 'U Turn'. So Bhau, more out of habit, drove on the wrong side, not realizing how drunk he was. With cars zipping across the highway, an unsteady Bhau could not control the bike when it suddenly swerved into the centre of the road, landing right in front of an oncoming car. Such was the impact that it threw Bhau onto the windshield of the car.

The head-on collision had damaged Bhau's bike completely, while the front end of the car was crushed.

The wife of the driver, who was sitting next to him in the car, had not been wearing a seat belt. Her face was damaged beyond recognition. The last we had heard was that she was still in a critical condition.

The car owner insisted on taking Bhau to court. He wanted justice.

It had taken only one bad night to change things forever. Life is but a thread knotting with many others: one wrong knot and the pattern of its weave changes forever.

Was Subbu's driving the bike on the ill-fated night, the wrong knot in Bhau's life?

How else could one explain the sudden change of heart when Bhau gave the bike keys to Subbu.

Did Bhau know that he was going to meet with an accident? Was Bhau trying to save Subbu when he gave Subbu the keys in an attempt to delay the inevitable? There were hundreds of questions circulating in my mind, but life continued to move without waiting for me to find the answers.

∼

Aman listened carefully to Bhau's dad before promising that he would look into the problem.

Bhau's dad felt much better after the reassurance and went back to his son's bedside.

∼

Parag stayed back with Uncle that night, while Subbu and I drove back home. I collected the boxes in which Mom had packed food before leaving and promised to get some breakfast in the morning when I came down to pick up Parag before heading for office.

Bhau's dad thanked us profusely for all that we were doing before he let Subbu and me leave. Being the only person who knew how to drive, I was left to do all the driving. I quietly shut the door behind me and joined Subbu near the gate to the ward. We stopped at a corner store for a smoke. It felt good to feel the smoke enter my lungs as a gust of wind hit me.

∼

Aman visited our desks the next afternoon. He seemed to be in a great hurry and was also looking excited for some reason.

'The case against Bhau is now closed,' he blurted out, eyes shining with triumph.

We were both surprised and glad to hear that.

'What did you do?' I asked, wanting to know how Aman had accomplished the feat so easily.

'Oh nothing, it just took me a few calls. The police have now filed a case against the car owner. He did not have the proper documents in the car,' Aman said gleefully.

'What happened to the woman, his wife?' I enquired softly afraid that I would open the can of worms.

'Oh! She was not his wife; she was a prostitute. The man broke down in police custody and confessed, requesting them to keep the fact hidden from his family!' Aman replied without batting an eyelid.

'She was injured badly wasn't she?' I continued wanting to get to the bottom of the whole matter.

'Oh we paid her well. She probably is in some hospital getting treated, glad for all the money she has earned.' Aman added sounding perturbed by my relentless questioning.

I wondered what had happened to the poor lady. She had probably walked away unable to face the shame that would have befallen her. She had probably seen so much pain in life that the injuries from the accident no longer mattered. She would only wish for more humiliation if she stayed back hoping for justice.

'But he was not at fault. It was Bhau's fault as far as I can see,' I argued.

'Come on! Whose side are you on?' asked Aman before continuing, 'I had to bribe a few people. It cost me fifteen thousand and some connections to sort the whole affair.'

I stood there perplexed and shocked not knowing if this was really a cause for celebration.

I wondered, if it had been me driving the car instead of that ill-fated driver.

I wondered if this is all that it took to escape after committing a crime. I had mixed reactions about the whole affair, but my admiration for Aman grew. I wondered what it took to be him. I was enthralled by his self-confidence. Then I rationalized that the driver of the car probably deserved his fate for cheating on his wife and family.

I conveniently willed myself to forget about the lady.

~

That afternoon would probably be the one that the three of us would never forget no matter how much we wanted to. The afternoon had changed the equations between Subbu, Parag, Aman and me forever. The guys became more open to Aman, and we started enjoying his company. We agreed never to let Bhau learn what had transpired in between the fateful night and his recovery.

We guessed it was in their best interests to keep Bhau and his father in the dark as far as the police investigation was concerned.

Subbu, Parag and I paid Aman for all his expenses, never intending to mention them to Bhau or his family. The money was probably the least we could do for a friend. The fact that Bhau was on the way to recovery had already paid us back a million times over.

~

It was a month before Bhau had recovered enough to join office. We had struggled and fought, but finally met the month-end deadline for the first delivery. AM was pleased with the way things had gone. He had even praised us at the month-end team meeting. The client had been very happy with the delivery and had even agreed to sponsor the team on a fun trip.

Bhau joined us back at office in time for the trip.

~

This delivery had set a new benchmark for all future deliveries and AM had once again proved that he could beat the toughest of timelines and surprise his adversaries by the wonderful work he could put in. It was later that we had learnt that the shortened project timelines had been AM's doing and not the client's. AM had always thought that our project team could deliver much more than what we currently did and this was his way of proving it. He had been famous for such turnarounds and had earned quite a reputation for it. The last delivery we'd made had not only saved time and money for the client, but also added business benefits in terms of faster delivery into market.

On hindsight, I think it was probably a little too late for us to learn about AM's miracles. Things had gone beyond anyone's control and there was little that we could have done at that stage but to let the events unfold on their own accord.

In winning his little wars, AM had completely ignored the battle.

11

THE COMMUNICATION SESSION

On Monday we were back in office after the brief Sariska trip. It was back to the toil and labour, as the second batch of code had to be delivered in a little more than two months' time. Life got back to the groove. Bhau continued to display the same level of commitment that we had come to expect of him before the accident.

It turned out to be a busy time for all the team leaders and managers as well, as the annual appraisals loomed closer. They were busy deciding on whom to promote and what hike one deserved.

As the appraisal drew nearer, Bhau turned grumpier than ever before. Aman was taking control of the team. He had even taken a lead in the team meeting the previous week. AM had toned down since the trip to Sariska and did not interfere much with our work.

However, having Bhau back in the team meant that we had lesser work to do. It also meant that I was left with spare time for my dates with Rajni.

Rajni had also been very busy with her filler activities. The magazine she had been working on had made a splash the week before. There had also been a lot of noise around how good the training plan that Rajni and her team designed was. She was sure that she would be considered for a promotion this time around.

I wondered if that would change things between Rajni and me because I was sure to be given a miss when they discussed the promotions. I knew I'd be lucky just to be considered worthy of a hike.

~

Subbu and I had been discussing the recent invite we had received from HR for a communication session at India Habitat Centre. I had not seen Rajni since morning and felt a sudden urge to see her. I feigned tea as an excuse before heading to the coffee machine.

I met Aman at the coffee machine. He looked rather annoyed with something. I asked him if there was a problem, but he rudely brushed me aside. I was a little miffed at Aman's reaction, but later reconciled to the thought that all the extra work around appraisals had taken its toll on him. I could empathize with the short temper one got when one was overloaded with work. I was usually under a spell of such bad tempers when project deadlines loomed close by.

However, that evening I saw Aman and AM inside the meeting room involved in a heated debate.

AM's face was red with anger while Aman looked calm and collected. He even seemed to have a snotty smile on his face.

I stood there transfixed, watching the action unfold inside the meeting room, when I caught Aman's attention.

He glared at me. At that moment I felt that there was something wicked in the way Aman had looked towards me. I felt a little frightened and immediately beat a hasty retreat, not wanting to be caught in the fallout of their feud.

I hurried back to my seat and soon forgot about the incident and got busy with the work at hand. I did not think the incident was important enough to mention to the gang.

The next day when Aman visited my seat to check my availability to conduct an interview, he acted like there was nothing amiss. Since he did not mention the previous evening's incident I decided that it was in my best interests to keep mum. Instead we talked about the project for a while before I agreed to conduct a few interviews for him over the next week. I wondered why Aman selected me for taking the interviews but soon forgot about it.

I got back to work once Aman left, wanting to finish the module before we left for the communication session that afternoon.

The communication session was a quarterly event in our organization. It was more like a ball for most of us. The communication session was followed by dancing that was only surpassed in fun by the great food and drinks that were on offer.

The communication session was also considered an opportunity to meet the higher management and see them in action, but we cared little for their speeches. We would have loved to skip this half of the session had we been allowed to do so.

This month's communication session was to be held at India Habitat Centre on Lodhi road.

Every IT company has its version of a communication session. These sessions are meant to be platforms to highlight the company's achievements and to also give the employees a glimpse of what is to come. These sessions had begun with the belief that the employees would only be able to deliver successfully if they knew the bigger picture. Things had changed in many companies and the communication session remained a mere formality where entertainment was given more priority than the bigger picture. The communication sessions were now reduced to mere canvassing platforms for the new management initiatives.

It was not just the sessions that had changed, what had changed with them was the underlying principles that governed the companies. IT companies work as independent cocoons instead of single cohesive units that they had started as. A company was divided into teams that were asked to do what seemed like independent pieces of work. The teams fought among themselves to prove their superiority, forgetting that it was the same company they were working for. These cocoons soon became insulated civilizations that had little to do with their next door neighbours.

The division into independent teams had started with the intention of forming great teams for different technical domains. The technical domains were later replaced by business verticals and now things were at a stage where nobody understood or cared what the teams had initially stood for. The IT companies had harboured a belief that inter-team competition would do well for the company and the performance of individuals, forgetting the simple fact that strength lay in unity.

It is funny how none of the companies any longer speaks of itself as one complete unit; rather it prides itself for being a collection of different companies.

I hear from my friends in the IT industry that companies are now coming up with 'integration' or 'best practice' teams that are intended to act as middlemen in identifying the best practices of the other independent teams and spreading the use of such practices across the organization.

Only time will tell us where we are headed, but I am sure it will not be long before we see change.

We had been asked to assemble at the venue an hour before the event was scheduled to start. We had all taken our seats, but there was still some time before the event would begin. The head of our organization walked up to the stage and greeted us before asking for volunteers to take the stage and entertain the crowd for the next thirty minutes.

A few people took the bait and volunteered with jokes and songs.

I was left wondering about the thin line that separated the world of IT from the days in college. Most of the IT companies employed people straight from college. These employees had little time to learn about the work culture or the industry norms. They still continued to think that they were in a college of a different kind.

There were trainings that told these employees about the softwares they were to work on but none told them about what the real change in their lives had been. None of the trainings talked about the transition from college into the IT industry, which left most of the new employees free to experiment and fend for themselves. Some of them got acclimatized while others struggled.

One would find many initiatives in IT companies which would put colleges to shame in immaturity. These companies celebrated rose days, best smile days, Miss Beautiful and Mr Handsome days alongside client meetings, management reviews and designing complex architectures.

~

I always thought it was foolish of people to want to hog the limelight.

It is sometimes amazing how people love to make a fool of themselves in front of huge crowds. I call such people 'attention grabbers'. This probably was a wonderful example of SA (Self Advertising) gone bad or being implemented in the wrong way. These were people who had failed to realize their dreams of making it big on the world stage, I thought ruefully. Or perhaps I was trying to justify my lack of courage to stand up and take the stage.

~

I looked around the hall trying to spot Rajni. She was to come to the venue along with Payal in her car. I cursed Payal for owning a car and even more so for having brought the car to the office that day. If only Payal had left her car at home, Rajni would have probably travelled with me.

~

The meeting soon started, once all the smart people of our company let go of the limelight.

~

The head of our organization began with a presentation on how much we had achieved in the last quarter. The speech highlighted everything that we had achieved till then and also how we had expanded into the organization we currently were. It was a long and boring speech that was making me sleepy. I was finding it hard to endure and looked around. Bhau and Parag sat intently listening to every word that was being spoken. Subbu was busy fiddling with his mobile.

'We have made great progress during the past few months, and it is now five years since we started,' he announced. 'I think we need a celebration befitting this achievement. We are going to host a huge party in order to celebrate the event. I want us to use this event to remember all our wonderful achievements. We will also have people visiting us from our client companies. I want this event to be remembered as something special and hope that all of you will extend a hand in making it so. Last week when I was talking to Kiran (our HR head) we were trying to work out ways to make this event memorable when we came up with the idea of making a movie about the organization.

'The movie would showcase all the facets of our organization and speak about what we truly are. I know for the movie to be able to bring out what we expect from it, it must come right from the heart. It must be something that all of us can relate to and feel good about and hence it should be something that is made by you, as you are the heart and the true identity of this organization.

'I want three movies and am expecting volunteers for the same. One of these movies will be selected and showcased at the event to celebrate our achievement.

'Can I please ask for volunteers to come forward?' As he uttered these words, all eyes turned away from the stage towards the spectators.

I felt a sudden urge to stand up. I nudged Bhau and Parag hoping that they would stand up to bolster my courage.

'I volunteer,' said a voice from one of the front rows. The voice belonged to Aman Sharma.

'That is wonderful!' said the head.

'What is your name, young man?' he asked.

'I am Aman Sharma, sir,' Aman replied.

The auditorium broke into huge applause that reverberated through as Aman took his seat.

I felt a twinge of jealousy streak through me. There were other people who volunteered for the project, but I recognized none of the others.

After the meeting, Aman rushed over to where Parag, Subbu, Bhau and I were standing.

'Hey, guys! We will do it! We will show them that our team is the best,' Aman said.

We enjoyed the rest of the evening with dance and drinks forgetting all about Aman and the movie.

Bhau did not drink since he had to drive back home.

I had a glass of whisky. Bhau's accident had made us all very cautious about the amount we drank before we took the wheel. We left the venue late that night. It was a Friday, and we had the weekend to recover.

12

THE SHINING STARS

I had given little or no thought to my writing since my last story. So much had happened since I wrote it that I had completely forgotten the pleasure I derived from writing.

Rajni had read the story and had liked it a lot. She had been constantly egging me on to continue writing, but had soon given up seeing my lack of enthusiasm. She was busy with other things.

I was still to share my story with Bhau or Subbu. With Subbu I feared that he would make fun of me. As for Bhau, the thought of asking him never crossed my mind.

Things had moved on at office since my first meeting with AM. We had seen very little of KK during this period. Our project had been picked up along with a few other projects to be showcased in the company's quarterly *Hall of Fame* magazine.

The magazine recognized employee achievements and projects that had made the company proud. The magazine was sent out to a select group of clients apart from being circulated internally to highlight the work and the dedication of the team in meeting client commitments across our organization. This magazine from the company's perspective helped meet the advertising needs besides serving as a medium of encouragement for the employees.

I was very happy with the recognition our team was receiving. We had heard that the next issue of *Hall of Fame* would have an interview with AM along with an article about our project. I had also heard that the magazine would have the names and photos of all the team members alongside a few appreciatory words from our client.

Rajni's team had finally secured a project from a client in Chicago. She, along with Rajeev, Sandeep and a few other teammates, was flying to Chicago for a month. Two of Rajni's teammates would be staying back in Chicago beyond the month, to facilitate client interactions and delivery. Naturally there were many people in her team who were vying for the opportunity to stay back in Chicago, beyond the initial month.

Rajni herself had been offered the opportunity to stay back for the first six month period but she had refused because of her mother's ill health.

It made me sad to think that Rajni would be travelling for a month but the fact that she had refused the long term offer made up a little. However, she was very excited about the trip to Chicago and understandably proud of it too! Besides this was the first time she was travelling abroad and the prospect of seeing a foreign land seemed to fill her up with joy. She had come up with a list of things she was planning of do and buy when she was in Chicago.

She wanted to get herself a laptop, an ipod for her brother, perfume for her mother along with many other things.

It was little more than a week before Rajni was scheduled to fly for Chicago. She had been very busy with the trainings that the company had organized. These trainings were intended to make the team aware of the banking fundamentals, since they were flying out for a banking project. I was constantly trying to find excuses to spend time with her but found it very hard with both Ashish and Payal trying to take up all of her free time.

Ashish and Payal were to stay behind. So like me they were trying to spend as much time as possible with Rajni. Thankfully for me, Rajni had a training scheduled for the coming weekend and was coming to office. Therefore, I had convinced her to spend a few hours with me after the training.

I myself was torn between the various tasks I had been assigned at office and having to worry about Rajni's trip. I had even considered asking Rajni to refuse the offer to go to Chicago, but seeing her eagerness I decided not to drop the idea.

Last week AM had awarded me with a 'Certificate of Achievement' for the improvement I had displayed. It was a simple blue and white certificate with my name emblazoned on it, but it had worked wonders for my morale. I was filled with pride as my name had been called out during the team meeting to receive the certificate.

KK and Aman had congratulated me for the certificate but Subbu had seemed to be in a foul mood that day.

Over the weekend, Rajni was left with very little time after the training and all we managed to do was to take a short drive around the office. 'There are so many things that I need to buy,' she had told me excitedly. She was happy packing and making plans for the trip. As the weekend drew to a close, I was left thinking of ways to spend as much time as possible with Rajni during her last week before the trip.

I was eager to get to office on Monday. The thought of being around Rajni was a big incentive. Rajni had told me that she would be busy with the preparations and the trainings but I had convinced her that we could at least have lunch and coffee breaks together. I hated having to sit along with Payal and Ashish, but there was little I could do. Subbu, Bhau and Parag had refused to join me and I was left to endure Payal and Ashish's taunts just to have spent a few minutes with Rajni.

That morning I signed on to my machine and opened the mailbox. There was a meeting invite from Aman calling us for a discussion on plans to move forward with the movie. There was also a mail from Rajni. I opened it eagerly.

'Hi! Good morning! I thought I should greet you first today.

'Pata hai? I had a wonderful dream last night, I will tell you about it when we meet! And before I forget, I will be late in coming to office tomorrow, have an appointment at the embassy for the visa stamping. Rajeev told me that the rules have been changed and everyone applying for the visa needed to attend in-person the interview at the embassy.

'Chalo! Need to move now, it is time for the banking training, catch you at lunch.

'Take care!'

I sat wondering what Rajni's dream could have been. The clock showed 9.30 a.m. We still had quite a few hours till lunch.

Subbu had just walked into his cubicle.

'Good morning!' I greeted him. We spent the next few minutes discussing about what we had done over the weekend before getting back to our machines.

~

I opened the invite from Aman and pressed the accept tab on the top. I had mixed feelings about the movie. On one hand, I thought it was a complete waste of time for the organization, however, on the other I was excited about having to do something different from the routine coding work.

Bhau, I was sure, did not want to have anything to do with it. He loved coding too much to pay attention to movies. Parag too had been ambivalent about it till then. And Subbu had been sarcastic all along. He thought that the movie was one of the many organizational ideas that fail to take wings. He had laughed it all saying, 'You and your movie. The Managing Director will soon forget about it and that will be the last you hear of it!'

Thankfully, despite their reservations, everyone had accepted the invite from Aman. The meeting was in an hour's time, I got back to work wanting to finish as much as possible before the meeting.

An hour later we entered the meeting hall with mixed feelings.

'I am sure you have all guessed why we are here,' said Aman sounding excited. 'This is a very good opportunity for all of us to become famous. Because the only way to grow fast in an organization is by improving your image with the higher management. Once we complete this movie, which I am sure is going to be the best, everyone in the company will know us. Everyone from top to bottom will recognize us by our names. No one can, then, stop your promotions or take you for granted.' As Aman spoke the last sentence, he first looked at Bhau and then slowly shifted his glance to me.

He continued, 'I know you people are really creative. I have seen the talent you possess. This is the right time and the perfect opportunity to bring it out in the open.'

We spent another hour in the meeting room deciding how to move forward. When we finally left the room, we were still undecided about what we wanted to do. Bhau remained an antagonist, while Parag had changed his stance a little which was probably because he did not care for coding as much as Bhau did.

I got back to my desk and started writing to Rajni. I wanted to tell her everything about the movie and what we were planning to do. Rajni had just returned from the training for a break. She immediately replied to my mail sounding very excited. She was positive that we would do a great job. For some reason she'd always thought that I was very creative, and after my conversation with her I was completely convinced about the idea of making the film.

~

That evening Subbu, Parag, Bhau and I sat around the table in the canteen discussing on how best to go about the project.

Parag spoke first. 'First of all, we will need to get a video camera. Does anyone have one?'

'I do,' said Subbu before adding, 'but, I am not going to give it for the movie. Why don't you ask Aman to provide one?'

'Yes,' concurred Bhau, 'The company should provide us a camera. At least this way we will be sure that they are serious about it.'

I continued to scribble on my notepad, the various inputs from around the table.

I scribbled, 'Ask Aman for a camera.'

We talked for a few more minutes trying to decide what we should be covering in the movie, but, finally, having gone nowhere, we left for home.

~

On the way back home, I told Dad about our new movie initiative.

Dad replied with a curt, 'Good.'

It was hard to read much into Dad's reply. I could never understand when he was being appreciative and when he was putting me down. On most occasions he seemed busy thinking about his work and I wasn't even sure that he heard what I told him.

Mom on the other hand was always eager to hear news about my work but more often than not tried to bring in the topic of my marriage into our conversations.

After what seemed like a long time Dad enquired about Bhau and his recovery after the accident. He even asked me a few questions about Bhau's parents. We continued with the small talk even as I took the way towards our house. I was eager to please Dad and hoped that at some point he would ask me about the movie or work. I wanted to tell him about the certificate AM had awarded me for my good work and also about the article that was to appear in the *Hall of Fame* magazine.

Dad though continued asking small questions. He seemed

very withdrawn from our conversation, almost as if there was something else on his mind.

As we neared our house, he opened up with his thoughts 'Anup, your mother and I have been talking about your marriage. You are twenty-six now and I think this is the right age for marriage. We want to get you married by next year,' Dad said before pausing.

My head was reeling with various thoughts. I felt numb.

'Look where you are going!' shouted Dad as the car swerved onto the pavement.

I quickly turned the steering wheel, trying to regain control of the car.

'But, Dad, I need some more time,' I meekly countered after having regained control of the car and myself.

I braced myself for what was coming next. I knew that once we got home it was going to be Dad and Mom against my lone voice.

I was yet to tell my parents about Rajni.

That night I called up Subbu and told him about our conversation.

Subbu laughed out loud before adding, 'Looks like your parents have more sense then you! Get married to the girl your Dad wants you to marry and live happily ever after. Forget about Rajni!'

~

Dad and Mom had been talking about my marriage for a few months before they had broached the subject openly in front of me. Like all other Indian parents they wanted to see their son happily married. Like all, they wanted the best girl for their son. And like many other Indian parents, they believed that the best girl, who would be the most suited for their son's hand, was to be found in the caste they belonged to.

There was nothing wrong with my parents' beliefs or intentions. It was strange that even as we had entered the twenty-first century, our country still reeled under caste-based prejudices. A country with one of the highest GDP growth rates in the world still looked down on people who belonged to lower castes.

We hankered about how the West discriminated against the blacks and the coloured, little realizing that an Indian was discriminated more at home than anywhere else. It is common, even today, to read news of brother or father killing their sibling or daughter because she had the courage to marry against the will of the family, because she had brought disgrace to the family by marrying out of caste.

In India it is common for people to be denied entry into a place of worship because they do not belong to a particular caste. In a country that prides itself for having shared the teachings from Vedas to the world, people still continue to believe prejudices against castes to be God's will.

~

The next day when we met during the coffee break, I shared what had happened at home, with Rajni.

'Oh, this has been going on in my house for a year now,' replied Rajni nonchalantly. 'All you need to do is cooperate with your parents,' she added.

I looked at her in astonishment.

She smiled before continuing, 'Tell your parents to start

looking for a girl. You can have some fun by adding bits about your preferences on the type of girl you want. Believe me, it takes a lot of time, and you always have the liberty of rejecting the first few proposals. And who knows, you might end up finding someone who is better than me,' she said shrugging and smiling.

I wondered about what Rajni had just said. Maybe she had a point.

Then suddenly she said, 'It is I who is going to have troubles,' looking sad for the first time since our conversation had begun.

I was looking for words to comfort Rajni but she started speaking again before I could manage anything. 'The trip to Chicago was a godsend for me. My parents had been insisting on moving forward with a proposal from a rich family who are connected with Dad through business. I wish I could have accepted the offer for the long term stay in Chicago. If only Mom had not fallen sick,' she said looking down at the table.

For a while she seemed to be lost in her thoughts, far away, thinking about the troubles at home. I moved my hand closer to hers to console her, not knowing what to say. My touch made her come back to the present immediately. She recoiled from my touch pulling her hand away from mine.

'Anup! This is office!' Rajni hissed angrily. There was an uncomfortable silence before Rajni started speaking again. 'Yesterday I heard Dad and Mom speaking about the proposal. They seem to have made up their minds and wanted to convince me that it was in my best interests to get married to this guy. Dad had told Mom that she was pampering me and my sister by letting us have our free

will. Dad had reasoned that all girls were against marriage
till they tied the knot. It was the pain of having to leave
their family that made them reluctant to marry. Once they
get married, it would all work out,' Rajni paused for a
while thinking about the incident before continuing.

'They are going to talk to me soon about it. Dad wants
me married by the end of this year. He wants to hurry
with the marriage, since my grandmother is in frail health
and if something happens to her, the marriage will need
to be put off for another year.' I could see the tears
welling up in her eyes.

I wondered what our fates had in store for us. I also
realized the fragility of our relationship. I realized that we
may never get married!

'Rajni,' I said pausing to get her attention before
adding, 'let us elope!'

She probably thought that I was joking because she
suddenly broke into laughter.

'Anup you are such a coward,' she said in a taunting
voice.

I was finding it difficult to understand her reaction.

'You know what I dreamt about yesterday?' she asked
and then without waiting for my reply said, 'I dreamt that
we were getting married at a temple. Our parents were
missing from the marriage, but my cousin brother Vishnu
was there helping us with the formalities. I was wearing a
beautiful red saree and you looked handsome in a cream
sherwani.' She sounded very excited.

I wondered how Rajni could forget her pain and find
solace in the silly dream.

'Anup, you know, most of my morning dreams have so
far come true.'

I was confused whether to draw comfort from Rajni's dream or to start willing her to begin the battle that had long been in waiting.

'You know I dreamt about meeting a south Indian guy and falling in love with him before meeting you.' Then suddenly she asked, 'Did you have a girlfriend before you met me?'

Rajni's question caught me by surprise. I was unsure whether to answer her truthfully or lie to her. I knew Rajni was very possessive and probably did not really want to hear the truth. I also knew that I could never lie to her.

'Yes, I did,' I replied before adding 'but it was only for a short while. We broke up within six months.' I waited for Rajni's reaction.

'*Dekha!* I even dreamt that you had a girlfriend before me. See, did I not tell you that my dreams have a habit of coming true!' There was a gleam in her eyes.

We spoke for a few more minutes before Rajni had to leave for her training. I was very glad that we had talked so openly. I was happier still because Payal and Ashish were not in office. Both of them had called in sick.

I went back to my seat, thinking about Rajni's dream and our destiny. The talk had been emotionally disturbing for I was lost between feeling happy, relived and sad. I quickly wiped the tears from my eyes hoping that no one had noticed me.

I wished fervently that I could make Rajni mine. I wished I could have her for myself and keep her safe, away from the pains of the world.

The rest of my day passed in coding.

Rajni had joined Subbu, Bhau, Parag, Nidhi and me for lunch since Payal and Ashish were on leave. She had to leave early that day to complete her shopping. Her interview at the embassy had gone off well and she was hoping to get the visa formalities completed before the weekend.

I was very glad for Rajni. I was happy the way things had turned out by the end of the day. As evening drove close, I found myself thinking about Rajni's dream and also hoping that like all her other morning dreams this one would also come true.

'Let's go for the meeting,' said Subbu whose sudden appearance broke my chain of thought.

I looked around perplexed. It was around 6.00 in the evening.

'What meeting?' I inquired.

'The movie meeting with Aman. Don't you remember we had decided to shift the meeting to after office hours so that it did not have an impact on the project,' replied Subbu annoyed at my question.

I quickly locked my machine before joining the others who were already walking towards Austin.

This was our second meeting to discuss the movie. We had not made much progress, apart from the fact that Aman had volunteered his camera for the movie. We were still to come up with a theme.

Aman had decided that since we had little time, it was important to have a daily update meeting to discuss the progress. We had decided in the last meeting that the best time for the daily meetings was after 6.00 p.m. when everyone had left for the day. This way we would not risk impacting the project deadlines.

The due date for the second batch of code was nearing, and we had a lot of coding to do. Bhau was working like a machine but was still left with a lot to do. It was hard to find time for the movie, but we had to somehow. Bhau had not come out openly against the movie, but we could sense his anguish about the whole affair. He feared that it would impact his already bleak chances of a promotion, if he came out strongly against the movie.

The meeting had been more or less fruitless with no sign of the theme in sight. We had decided that the script would revolve around the company's vision and achievements. We also wanted to include the tag line of our company—'We build relationships, products just happen'—as the main theme for the movie.

'It should be something that revolves around Training, Caring, Sustaining and Protecting,' said Parag helping us recollect what our company stood for.

Aman had hardly spoken. He spoke as we got ready to leave. It had been an hour since the meeting had started.

'I have a very busy week ahead and probably will not be able to join you in the next few meetings. I will try and make it as and when I can but do keep me included in all the mails and also send me regular updates,' said Aman.

We moved out of the meeting room.

Subbu whispered into my ears, 'Ah! Now that is a better way of telling us that you can do all the work while I enjoy the benefits!'

'Shut up Subbu! He must really be very busy,' I replied tartly before making way to my desk.

Subbu was always very pessimistic, I thought to myself before setting off for home.

~

It had been three days since we had started working on the movie.

I had reached office an hour back and was trying to finish the changes that Bhau had suggested after reviewing my module.

'Anup, can you come with me?' I heard a voice calling for me. I raised my head away from the lines of COBOL. It was Aman. He had been waiting for me. I stood up slowly, and followed him after locking my machine. It was dangerous to leave the machine unlocked when Subbu was around. Last time I had forgotten to lock my machine, Subbu had sent around an email to our entire group with a subject line that read: 'I am beautiful . . .'

People pulled my leg for weeks after the incident.

Aman spoke again as we neared the lift, 'Anup, I want you to do an interview for me.'

'But, Aman, I am not prepared. I have never done an interview. Can't you ask Bhau?'

'Oh shut up! You don't need to prepare for an interview. I am sure you will manage,' Aman laughed patting my shoulder as he said that.

I followed Aman into the lift feeling uneasy. And while we waited for the lift to reach the ground floor, I wondered why Aman had selected me for conducting the interview.

As we exited the lift, Aman looked towards Anjali, who immediately pointed to the visitors' room. There was no exchange of words. Anjali had probably been waiting for Aman to come down to interview the candidate. We walked into the visitors' room to meet the interviewee.

After the initial introductions, I started with my first interview. I spent the next few minutes asking questions that sometimes failed to make much sense, even to myself. I wondered what was going through the interviewee's head. Nevertheless, I wanted to impress AM and continued asking things that even I did not have the answers to. I probably was going to end up making a fool of myself but there was not much I could do otherwise.

Thankfully for me, the candidate wasn't very bright. He seemed to be unable to answer even the simplest of questions. The complicated ones totally baffled him. His inability to answer gave me a false sense of satisfaction. It gave me an illusion that I was doing a wonderful job. Few minutes into the interview I seemed to have asked everything that I knew or could recollect.

I was on the verge of asking my twenty-fifth question when Aman spoke, 'I think that is enough, Anup. Let us leave him alone now. I think you have already asked him everything we wanted to know.'

We walked out of the visitor's room, promising the candidate that someone would contact him soon.

I was worried that Aman was upset with the way the interview had gone. He walked into the adjacent room while I followed him meekly. Once inside, Aman praised me for the way things had gone with the interview. He told me that he looked forward to me conducting many more interviews for him. I felt much better on hearing Aman's praises. I probably had not done such a bad job with the questions after all, I thought.

'So, what do you think about the candidate?' Aman asked.

'I think we should not hire him,' I replied before adding, 'He did not answer a single question convincingly.'

'Ah! I did notice that,' said Aman, 'but I think he has lot of potential. He has done wonderfully in our aptitude test. It is probably just that he has not been doing the type of work you people are used to.'

I wondered if that was true, the candidate had not even answered basic questions around COBOL.

'He also has an excellent academic background,' Aman added as an afterthought.

'But Aman, our aptitude test is very simple. It is quite possible that he got the question paper through someone who had written the test before him. I think everyone in the job market knows the questions they ask in our aptitude tests,' I retorted.

'You are being very pessimistic Anup. I interviewed him before you came down. He was wonderful,' Aman sounded annoyed as he said this.

Aman then asked me to fill out the review sheet and sign it. He also made sure that I gave the candidate an above average rating.

I walked back to my seat, not really sure of what had transpired.

I spoke little about the incident to Bhau, Subbu and Parag, fearing that I would end up making a fool of myself. I had no experience with interviews and thought that I was probably a little too harsh on the candidate. Aman was more mature and experienced. Then I got back to my code, hoping to finish it before we had to leave for the movie meeting in the evening.

～

Rajni's friends, Ashish and Payal, were back from their sick leave.

I knew there would be a lot that Payal and Ashish would want to share with Rajni and hence stayed away from Rajni that day. The only time Rajni and I met was during the lunch hour. I missed the time when I had lunch with Bhau, Subbu and Parag.

Rajni did mention a few times that I should stop punishing myself by having lunch with her group and do what I liked, but like most things that are associated with the heart, the lunch was a big sacrifice I was forced into. What I hated more than the lunch was, having to go out for a walk with Rajni's group. It was not just the childish prattle and the useless banter that annoyed me, it was also Ashish's antics that frustrated me.

I feigned a telephone call and bid farewell to Rajni and her group at the company gate that afternoon, before beating a hasty retreat to my desk. Subbu and Bhau were occupied with the coding. Parag seemed to be busy on the phone.

AM had sent around a mailer asking for the progress we were making with our modules. I spent the next few minutes replying to AM's mail.

It is funny how quickly time passes when you have a lot of work to do. I was surprised when it was 6.00 p.m.

13

CHICAGO

The days just whizzed past with meetings for the film and a huge amount of coding that we had to do for the next delivery. It was Friday even before we had an opportunity to blink.

Rajni's tickets for Chicago had been booked for the weekend. She was to fly out of Delhi on Sunday, early morning at 2.45. She was on her way down to collect her passport and the traveller's cheques when I met her near the coffee machine. For some reason Rajni looked anxious. I could even see the sadness in her eyes. I wondered if it had something to do with being away from me for a month. The thought of asking Rajni about this did cross my mind more than once, but my uncertainty about her reply forced me to curb my eagerness.

'Why are you looking so worried, baba?' I asked her lightly as she waited for the lift.

'Nothing,' she replied putting on an air of nonchalance that she usually did when she wanted to hide her true feelings.

'Can we go out for a short drive today?' I enquired, ignoring her reply. 'We will not be able to meet again till you are back from Chicago and you don't even want me to come to the airport,' I added pleading with a hope that Rajni would condescend.

'*Nahin*! I don't think it is possible today, there is so much I still need to do,' replied Rajni as the lift opened. Then just as an afterthought she added, 'Okay, let me see if we can, may be go out for a little while in the evening,' as she entered the lift.

I walked back to my seat wondering about the long month that awaited me. I knew it was going to be very hard without Rajni around. Then I remembered the conversation we had had about her dream of our marriage. The thought gave me a lot of comfort. However, I saw very little of Rajni that day after our meeting near the coffee machine. When she was not held up by the forms she was busy consoling Payal and Ashish. I felt a pang of jealousy seeing her spend so much time with them. Time had also worked against me. It was 5.30 p.m. when Rajni finally finished all her work; too late to go out for a drive—I felt annoyed with Rajni. The pain of parting with her for a month seemed to make me even angrier. Subsequently, when it was finally time for Rajni to leave for the day, I was too annoyed to even wish her the best for her journey. I felt sorry for Rajni and myself and wished I could have forced myself to act a little less conceited.

My thoughts were still with Rajni when it was time for our daily movie meeting. It had been a week since the communication meeting. We had not made much progress with the movie. Aman was getting frustrated. There were many ideas on the table, but there were none that all of us agreed on. We knew we had to decide soon.

~

It was Saturday evening. I lay on my bed listening to Kenny G, wondering what Rajni would be doing at the moment. Probably, on her way to the airport. I had found myself listening to Kenny G a lot since Rajni and I begun dating. The *Joy of life, Forever in love* had become a part of my life just as much as *Jasmine flower* and *The wedding song* had. I would spend endless hours sitting in my room listening to Kenny G as I lived and relived all the moments with Rajni. The dreams of future with her were now entwined into the songs in the album *Breathless*. The music not only helped soothe my nerves during hard times but also made me loose myself to my dreams.

I must have fallen asleep listening to the soothing music when I was woken up at midnight by a noise. I jumped up in shock and realizing where the noise had come from rushed to the music player to turn it off. It had begun playing the next CD once Kenny G had completed his time on air. The volume of the player, though low, had been loud enough for a shrill Hindi movie song.

Being rudely awoken, I realized I could not go back to sleep immediately. I sat on the bed recollecting my thoughts for a long time and slowly things started falling into place. I pulled out my notepad and started writing.

I wondered if I saw the sequence in my dreams when I had fallen asleep or if I had thought it all out just then while sitting on my bed. It really did not matter. I scribbled hurriedly on the notepad lest I forgot:

SCENE-I

The camera rolls making way for a little kid walking into the scene, the kid is still learning to walk. He stumbles and his mother rushes in. She holds the child, helping him to walk as letters forming 'LEARNING' slowly appear on the screen.

The camera rolls through the various training sessions and induction programmes showing employees having fun, pulling pranks and learning at the same time.

SCENE-II

The scene starts with the sun rising above the horizon as the camera slowly turns to a football field. A group of children are playing when one of them suddenly falls down and hurts himself. The mother of the child runs to his aid and brushes the wound before kissing the forehead as the letters 'CARING' slowly appear on the background.

The camera rolls towards the canteen, gymnasium and various parties showing employees during various times of the day.

SCENE—III

This scene starts with a wall in the foreground. Then a child comes into the picture. He is attempting to walk on it. His mother with outstretched arms is beside him, in case he falls. The letters 'PROTECTING' appear on the screen.

The camera rolls, showing employees working on various social causes. The scene revolves around the people whose life the company had changed through various charity initiatives.

The scene ends at a foster home that had been recently adopted by our organization.

The movie finally ends with the company mission statement, 'We build relationships, products just happen' scrolling on the picture.

My excitement grew as I continued scribbling. After finishing I slowly formulated my thoughts putting the scenes into place, mentally picturing how they would appear. Since I was eager to share my thoughts with someone, I picked up my mobile and dialled Parag's number. After five attempts, I succeeded in reaching him.

'Helloooo, who is this?' answered Parag groggily.

I spent the next fifteen minutes explaining my idea to Parag which he probably understood little of but was forced by my enthusiasm to continue listening. He finally agreed that it was a great idea and suggested that we discuss it in the next day's meeting.

I spent another hour working on the script before getting ready for bed. I doubted if I would be able to get much sleep before morning. I could not wait for the movie meeting next day.

I had just switched off the lights when I heard my phone buzzing. I quickly switched the lights back on before rushing to the phone, wondering who could be calling so late in the night. I thought it was probably Parag wanting to add something to the script but was surprised to see Rajni's name flash on the mobile screen.

I disconnected her call and redialled her number, wondering if she was calling from the flight cabin itself, now that the flight was due to depart. Rajni promptly responded.

'Hello,' I said still trying to reorganize my thoughts. It was 3.00 in the morning.

'Anup!' said Rajni. I could make out that she was close to tears. My heart started beating as I worked out the various possibilities and was still struggling to find words when Rajni spoke again.

'Anup, our trip has been cancelled!' she added before pausing to blow her nose. This came as a shock to me. My first impulse was an intense desire to be able take Rajni in my arms and letting her know that everything would be fine; she went on explaining in a flood of tears.

'Jiten called Rajeev a few hours back and asked him not to check in. We had been waiting at the counters for our turn to check in when Rajeev shared this news with us. Initially I thought that Rajeev was joking but when he persisted and asked us to verify the news with Jiten, I was sure he was telling us the truth.'

Jiten worked in the administration department of our organization.

I tried consoling Rajni for there was little I could do sitting at home. 'Where are you now?' I finally managed to ask, after Rajni's sobs had subsided a little.

'I have called Dad. My parents were on the way, returning home from the airport. Dad said he will be at the airport in five minutes,' Rajni seemed to have gained control over herself after the initial breakdown. We spoke for a few more minutes before her parents finally arrived. I made a few calls to my other friends on Sunday in order to understand what had happened but there was little they could tell me.

I anxiously waited for Monday when I could go into office and learn from Rajni first-hand about the whole affair.

Dad was surprised that I was ready long before him that morning. I was both anxious and excited as we drove to the office. My anxiety was about Rajni and the excitement was obviously about sharing the script of the movie with others. In my dazed state I even managed to drive without swearing at the insane traffic.

Once in the office, I sneaked a peek towards Rajni's cubicle as I exited from the lift. She was yet to come in. I walked to my desk a little disheartened. It could be a long wait. Then once I logged on to my machine, my excitement about the script got the better of me. I emailed my idea to everyone including Rajni and waited for their comments, or rather praises, to trickle in.

Parag loved what I had written and so did Bhau. Surprisingly, even Subbu liked it. I didn't hear from Aman. He was probably busy in some meeting. I anxiously waited for the movie meeting that evening.

~

It was nearly 11.00 a.m., Rajni had still not replied to my mails. I walked round the lift to check on her but she was still not in for the day. Then I spotted Rajeev at his desk and walked across to where he sat wanting to know what happened to the trip. The trip, I learnt, had been cancelled because apparently the client had developed cold feet and pulled out at the last moment. Moreover, the US market had suddenly slumped and the client no longer wanted to invest in the new software. Our company till late into Saturday had been working on various options to convince the client to go ahead with the project. They had finally given up looking at the persistent reluctance of the client. It was late in the night when the final decision to call off the trip had been taken. And even though there had been a major concern about employee morale, the management claimed its helplessness. Rajeev and the others had been promised a trip as soon as an opportunity presented itself, but that was of little consolation.

I wanted to call Rajni and share what I had learnt with her, but could not get myself to call her.

~

Around noon, I got a reply from Aman: 'Theme is okay, but could have been a little more innovative. I think we can do something better,' was all he had written in his mail. Disheartened at my efforts going unappreciated, I forwarded his mail to Parag, Subbu and Bhau. I was thinking about how I could improve on the story, when Parag walked over to my desk.

'Hey, cheer up man! Don't read too much into that idiot's reply. Or better still do one thing—you let me handle this. Don't speak in the meeting until spoken to, and I will do the rest,' he instructed sounding his confident self.

It looked like Parag had a plan and having nothing better in mind, I agreed.

~

There was still no sign of Rajni. I got busy working on the modules forgetting all about her and the script. Soon it was that time of the day. The four of us streamed into the meeting room. Aman was already there. Previously, Aman had been infrequent with the meetings. I was not sure if he was going to make it today. But then he had probably realized that this meeting was going to be an

important one since we were close to formalizing the
script. Aman, I guessed, did not want to be left out when
the important decision was made. He wanted to be sure
that the movie was progressing well but more so to ensure
that his inputs for the movie were considered. He looked
annoyed about something. Probably he had been having a
bad day at office. It was understandable since he had to put
up with both AM and KK. I felt sorry for him wondering
how he managed.

We had just taken our seats and were waiting for the
meeting to begin when Parag started speaking even before
anyone of us had an opportunity to speak.

'Aman, I am glad that we finally have a plan. I must say
it was possible only because of the lead you provided in
the last meeting,' started Parag sounding very confident. I
was not sure about what he was playing at, but looking at
his confidence my faith grew. Also, for the first time since
the meeting had started, Aman began to look interested.

Bhau and Subbu looked equally puzzled about the
whole affair. Parag continued, 'Aman had mentioned that
we should make a movie about the company ethics and
beliefs. The movie should speak for the employees and the
achievements of the company during the last five years.
Aman had also added that we should have interesting bits
in the movie. And that it should be hilarious and, at the
same time, cover all the aspects of the company.'

Parag paused before turning to Aman for confirmation.
Aman nodded, agreeing with what Parag had said. I
realized that these were comments that Aman could hardly
deny!

Parag continued, 'I think the script that Anup sent
around this morning is exactly what Aman had suggested.

Anup, is that not so?' Parag continued, not waiting for my reply. 'I think Anup's idea is just a combination of Aman's individual suggestions. I think, Anup, you were great in combining all the plans Aman suggested.' By now, Parag had Aman completely at his mercy. I nodded in agreement as the meeting moved on.

It was one of the fastest agreements ever to be reached for a movie script.

Other than a few, minor changes Aman finally agreed to it. Once the script had been finalized, he left the meeting saying that he had some other important meetings to attend. Before leaving, he thanked us for the excellent work we were doing and promised us that we would be rewarded aptly for our efforts!

~

Later that evening Parag and I got to discuss what had happened in the meeting. Parag had gauged from my expressions that I was not very happy about the way things had gone. Parag counselled me that this was our movie, and it hardly mattered if Aman thought the story was his. Parag's argument was that, since we were all in it, it would be the team that should look for the credit and not the individuals. Parag added that if I was still annoyed about my script no longer being mine then I was not acting like a team player. By the time we finished, I agreed with and accepted Parag's line of thought.

~

Our meeting had continued after Aman had left the meeting room. We discussed the dates and other requirements.

'I think since the movie will only last for ten minutes we don't have enough time to cover everything in the story. We would be showing the movie in snippets and it is best we make use of subtitles and probably an anchor who could help in conveying what we are trying to express,' suggested Parag. Everyone seemed to agree with Parag. It really made sense since it was impossible to cover all the aspects in ten minutes and yet successfully communicate everything we intended to.

'Hey, Anup, why don't you start? Let us see how you look on the camera,' urged Parag. I was surprised by the sudden suggestion. I stood up a little shakily, after all my protests had failed. Subbu was ready with the camera as I started speaking.

'Hi and welcome to . . .' I stopped before uneasily looking at the others.

'Welcome to what? Don't we have to decide on the details of the script? Come on! I can't do it without a script,' I said before heading back to my seat. All of us, including Subbu, tried our luck at being an anchor but failed miserably. Now it was Parag's turn.

Parag looked deeply involved in something. He looked up before starting. 'I don't think this is going to work out. Who the hell would want to watch a movie with boring people like us in it? Let me tell you, if this has to work, we need to find a female anchor. It will not only add lustre to the movie but also make it interesting and pleasant to watch.'

After a few mild protests, we all agreed with what Parag had suggested. We went back to the drawing board, trying to decide who the right person would be.

'Priyanka,' Subbu suggested helpfully.

'Hey, not Priyanka!' retorted Parag. 'She is too beautiful and also very conceited. Besides she is not a team player,' he added.

We worked through all the other names that came to our mind. We even considered Payal, but were unanimous in our decision that she would be our last choice. It was after many arguments and lot of thought that we settled on Nidhi.

Looking back, I think this was a masterstroke of destiny. Nidhi was the best thing that could have happened to the movie. She was more than just beautiful, unlike girls like Priyanka and Payal. She was very charming, down to earth and really pleasant to watch. She had an equally beautiful voice and carried herself really well.

I still remember what Parag had said when he had first seen Nidhi in office—'She has eyes to die for.' I could not agree more.

In short, I think this was when our movie moved from being just mediocre to great.

Parag wanted me to approach Nidhi since I already knew her well through Rajni. I was a little reluctant because I was not sure if Rajni would appreciate the idea. I also feared that Rajni would assume that it had been my brainwave to consider Nidhi for the role. So I had to steer clear of controversy. We were also sure that Subbu was the last person who should be speaking to Nidhi, which left Bhau and Parag. In reality, it just left Parag because Bhau could be an expert with computers, but when it came to girls, he developed cold feet.

The other reason that had worked against Bhau was the fact that he was yet not completely convinced about the idea of the film—he still thought it was the most foolish thing to do.

14

THE PERFECT SCENE

Parag finally agreed to speak to Nidhi about the movie in the evening. It was nearly eight by the time we left the meeting room that day. I was very pleased with the progress we had made with the movie. We finally had a script to work on—now all we needed were the stars.

~

The next day I was busy working on the modules at my desk when Ashish came down to my seat.

'Anup,' he said, waiting for me to look up at him before continuing, 'Rajni called me up this morning. She said she would not be coming in this week.' Ashish seemed to be relishing my discomfort. He waited for the news to sink in before adding, 'She asked me to inform you that she did not want you calling her for the next few days.'

I was sure he was enjoying himself as he gave me the news from Rajni. I wasn't sure why Rajni had selected him as the messenger. Why couldn't she have asked Payal? As I sat at my desk seething with anger, Ashish stood by

my side looking down at me for what seemed like
eternity, patiently waiting for my reply. I continued to
ignore him while trying hard to concentrate on the
modules. Realizing the futility of standing by me, he soon
walked away, but I was sure I had seen a grin on his face!

~

It had not been easy convincing Nidhi. She had been very
reluctant to face the camera and had only agreed after
much persuasion from Parag and myself. Initially she was
a little shy and stuttered while she spoke. She was a little
too conscious of the surroundings. It took a lot of
convincing and guidance from Parag before Nidhi could
even utter a line convincingly on camera. Thankfully the
one thing that Parag did not lack during those days was
patience.

We were soon beginning to realize that shooting the
movie was not going to be as easy as we had initially
imagined. It was not easy to emote with all eyes, including
the camera's, looking at you. However, Nidhi was slowly
but steadily getting better.

I recall how much we learnt during those initial days.

Bhau had also begun to take interest in the movie. His
training in photography from his engineering days at Pilani
seemed to be coming back to him as he struggled with the
angles and the lighting. Subbu, who had initially taken up
the baton as our cameraman, had reluctantly handed over
the camera to Bhau. And being the perfectionist that he
was, Bhau even pulled out his books from days at college
to look up the notes from his training.

Things got much tougher for Nidhi also, with Bhau
behind the camera. She needed to try harder to get the

scenes to Bhau's satisfaction. She even broke down a few times in frustration, unable to put up with Bhau's attitude. It was only after Parag had stepped in to cool matters that she reluctantly agreed to continue. She was definitely not a natural.

Things sometimes reached a situation where we were forced to rethink about our decision to persist with Nidhi. It was only because of Parag's obstinacy that we agreed to continue with her. Parag spent hours with her trying to help her hone her skills. And soon the evidence was there for all to see.

Surprisingly, through all the melodrama around the movie, it completely failed to dawn on Subbu and me that there was much more cooking between Parag and Nidhi!

The camera and Nidhi soon became less of a worry. The only concern that remained was about shooting the scenes.

It was already Thursday, three days since my conversation with Ashish. I was still very annoyed with Rajni. The last thing I wanted to do was to speak with her. We were in the conference room looking at the scenes we had shot the previous day. We were not very happy with what we saw. The results on the television had left us dismayed. The only consolation, if any, was the fact that Nidhi seemed much more confident in front of the camera since the time we had started.

Nidhi had work to catch up on that evening and had left early. It was just Subbu, Parag, Bhau and me at the meeting.

'Anup, I think Nidhi would look much better with a little make-up,' said Subbu looking closely at the scene playing on the television. 'You can see the light shinning on her face, there is so much perspiration. We should probably give it a thought when we shoot next.' Subbu added before continuing 'It would help if you could tell her to wear something in softer shades. Something that is more appropriate for the scene.' Subbu was looking at me as he spoke.

'How can I tell her something like that?' I replied annoyed with Subbu singling me out.

The room went silent as Subbu hit the rewind button and played the scene back.

It was apparent that someone had to speak to Nidhi about her dress and make-up. The question was who could do that without hurting Nidhi or making her feel uncomfortable.

'Someone has to do it. It will make the scenes much better,' said Parag after we had watched the shot for the second time. 'Why don't you ask Rajni to help?' he suggested. 'I am sure Rajni can speak to Nidhi about it without making Nidhi feel uncomfortable.'

I recollected my conversation with Ashish at the mention of Rajni's name. The more I thought about the conversation the more I hated Rajni. It pained me when I thought about what had passed between Ashish and me that day. I failed to understand why Rajni had to ask Ashish to do her bidding. Did she not know how much I hated Ashish? What could be more demeaning then letting Ashish prove that he was closer to Rajni than I was?

It was not just my ego that had taken a beating that day. Rajni had breathed life into a doubt that had lurked in my mind, making an appearance every time I saw Ashish and her together. I was in pain every time I recollected the conversation with Ashish. Rage pulled at my heart strings making it difficult for me to breathe. It was like a lump that had stuck in my throat, refusing to move up or down. A strange situation stared me in the face. The last thing I wanted to do was to talk to Rajni. I was furious at Rajni and yet I knew my heart longed to be close to her. I knew that deep inside me, I prayed that things were back on an even keel between the two of us. No matter how hard my brain tried to convince me otherwise, in my heart I continued to believe that Rajni was mine.

I stood there embroiled in my thoughts staring down at the floor. I knew it would not be long before I broke down, unable to bear the pain. It was as if on cue my phone started vibrating. The phone probably wanted to save me from the shame of breaking down in front of my friends.

I excused myself before exiting the conference room. The phone had stopped ringing as soon I closed the door behind me. I looked at the screen wondering who it was that had been calling me.

'1 missed call Rajni' was displayed on the screen. I walked towards the restroom fighting my urge to call Rajni back. I was determined not to talk to her. The phone buzzed again before going dead. I did not bother checking who it was knowing it to be Rajni. I entered the restroom and walked up to the basin. The tears that I was fighting hard to stop seemed to get a life as I watched the water flow from the tap. I cried as I repeatedly splashed my face with water. I stood there looking at my face in the mirror for a long time, before walking out of the restroom, feeling a little better. I walked towards the conference room still determined not to make the call.

I was about to enter the conference room when my

phone started buzzing again. This time the phone did not stop ringing after the first ring. I knew and hoped that it was Rajni. I was losing the battle. My heart was winning with every buzz the phone made. I finally accepted my defeat and walked across to the adjacent meeting room. I entered the meeting room and closed the door behind me. I did not bother with the lights as I picked up the call. The room was faintly lit from the street lights below. I could make out the shadow of the furniture as I walked towards the window.

'Why are you calling?' I hissed into the phone, still annoyed with the way Rajni had behaved. 'You can talk all you want to Ashish,' I added furiously. I wanted to bang the phone down, but could not get myself to do it. The pain in my chest welled as I fought the urge to let out my frustration. I had little choice as tears flowed out from my eyes. All the things that I had done for Rajni had come down to this, I wondered. I was sobbing into the phone.

'Anup! What is wrong?' said Rajni sounding concerned. 'Hey, it is just been four days! I thought I'd call you sooner but somehow I just could not seem to get over the fact that they cancelled my trip at the last moment,' she added.

'Why did you have to do this to me Rajni? Why?' I hissed back into the phone having gained my composure back. Then I looked around to make sure that no one was watching me.

I waited for Rajni's reply.

I knew our relationship would never be the same, but I wanted my answers before I let things go.

'What did I do?' said Rajni sounding innocent.

I spent the next few minutes recounting my conversation with Ashish.

Rajni listened quietly till I had finished. I was sure she was finding ways to make up to me, feeling sorry about what she had done, but I was determined not to let her win this time.

'Anup, will you now listen to me . . . please,' Rajni spoke after a long time. 'I did not call anyone. It was Ashish who called me up on Monday. I told him that I wasn't coming in for a week and did not wish anyone to call me up during that time. I had told Ashish this only for his and Payal's benefit,' Rajni paused. I heard her inhale deeply before continuing.

'I did not ask Ashish to tell you anything. I wanted to call you up the first thing, when I felt a little better. Then I thought it was best to let the pain subside before we spoke. I did not want you worrying for me. Why would I want Ashish to speak to you? I know how you feel about him.' She continued, 'I don't understand why Ashish did what he did and I don't want to know either. Please do me a favour, don't mention anything to him,' I could hear Rajni sniffling.

'But Rajni how was I supposed to know?' I asked after a long pause. I felt pain, happiness, relief and sorrow all at the same time.

'No, Anup it is not your fault, I don't blame you. I know you are a kid. I know how much you care for me and love me. I know how immature you can be sometimes. It is my fault. I should have known what I was getting into with you and Ashish,' Rajni seemed to be in pain as she spoke these words.

'Rajni I am really sorry,' I replied before adding, 'will

you please marry me? I know I am not perfect but I will never give you a reason to complain,' Rajni was still sniffling into the phone.

'Anup I know you won't give me a reason to complain. I frankly have nothing against you. I promise things will be much better for you henceforth, just give me a little time to think things over,' she said.

I did not know what to make out from the conversation. It was hard to understand what Rajni was feeling at the moment. I was afraid that Rajni had not understood me completely. I feared that I would lose my Rajni.

'Rajni can we meet today . . . please. I really want to see you,' I pleaded into the phone.

She laughed for the first time since she had called. 'Anup you are such a kid!' she said, sounding much better, but she had still not recovered completely. 'Chalo! Mom is calling me, I really need to go,' she added.

'Do you love me?' I asked wondering if Rajni still felt the same way about me.

There was a long pause before Rajni replied. 'Yes dear, I do. Love you . . . Love you . . . Love you . . .' she whispered before cutting the phone.

It was not joy I felt then . . . it was not happiness. What I felt could not be explained in words. As I walked out of the meeting room I felt as if I had conquered the world! I knew I could die a hundred times over just to hear Rajni say those three beautiful words!

~

When I finally went back to the conference room others had already wrapped up the meeting and left. I was relieved after the call from Rajni and had found a new energy to go ahead with the movie. I rushed back to my cubicle expecting the others to be still there.

I saw Subbu, Parag and Bhau huddled around Subbu's desk, and wondering what had caught the group's attention this time, I moved towards them. 'What is it guys?' I asked as I neared Subbu's desk.

'Oh! Don't worry it is just a reminder to fill in our objectives and self ratings for the appraisals,' said Subbu.

'I don't think we need to worry about filling it up, as things stand, there is little we can expect,' added Bhau helpfully.

'It is all hogwash anyway, there is nothing to appraisals other than making a fool out of you,' said Parag walking back to his cubicle to collect his things before leaving.

It was nearly eight at night when we finally left office.

I did not bother to check my mails before leaving office.

~

The annual appraisal appears like clockwork every year, causing unimaginable damage in their wake for a month before moving ahead. They are like the devastating hurricanes but just a little more predictable in terms of their occurrence.

There are certain standard steps for any appraisal cycle: The first step involves the employees rating themselves on their objectives set by the company followed by filling in justifications against the objectives stating the reasons for the ratings.

The employee then forwards the ratings to the manager.

Once the manager receives the objectives along with the self ratings from the employee, he schedules a

1–1 meeting. The manager rates the employee's objectives with what he thinks the employee truly deserves. The 1–1 is a stage for discussion between the manager and the employee, providing each with an opportunity to defend or agree with the final ratings.

However, one must add that the ratings from the managers invariably tend to be lower than the employee's self ratings. By the time sessions are done, the manager has either convinced the employee or forced him into accepting the ratings the manager thinks he deserves.

Then the manager forwards the final ratings and the objectives to the Human Resources team.

HR finally decides your fate based on these ratings.

There was not much to be expected in terms of rating if you worked for someone like AM. You could never aspire to reach up to AM's high standards, so there was little to be gained from filling up the innumerable forms trying to justify what you had done.

I prepared myself for the next 1–1 with AM. If my past experiences were anything to go by, the next session was definitely going to be painful.

~

It was Friday. The week had passed without much progress made on the movie front. Aman had joined us for the movie meeting that evening. We had informed him about our woes with the project work, the appraisals and the movie. Aman had shrugged it all off indifferently adding that the hard work would reap rewards for us if we stuck with it.

He was also not very happy with the bits and pieces we showed him from our shooting and reminded us of the impending deadline before adjourning the meeting. We just had three weeks for the movie and just about the same time for completing the appraisal process. The code delivery was scheduled for a week after the event where the movie would be showcased.

The next few weeks were going to be a nightmare to get through.

~

Saturday morning I sat in my room doing what I did best in times like these, listening to music. My thoughts were still with the movie script, wondering how I was going to change it into something more feasible. I did not want to change the main concept around which our initial idea had hovered. My thoughts were cut short by the music on the player. I pressed the pause button before replaying the tune. I listened to the tune about eight times before I knew what needed to be done.

I immediately called up Parag and asked him to reach office with the others.

That weekend we shot our first scene, the first few seconds of the movie. We roamed around the office corridors shooting the library, meeting rooms, cafeteria, recreational facilities and even the toilets, with first few seconds of the background music from *Eye of the tiger* soundtrack. We spent nearly four hours shooting the various facets of the office, before going to the conference room to review our handiwork. It was hard to visualize the final product without the music but we did our best.

That evening we left office at 7.00 having completed what we intended to shoot.

I spent the remaining part of my weekend on the

Movie Maker software trying to match the sound and the visuals. I spent hours editing and re-editing bits till I was satisfied with the scene. It was late at night on Sunday when I got the first thirty seconds of the movie ready. I could not wait to show it to the group.

Things started falling into place once we completed our first scene.

～

I entered office on Monday hoping to share the scene with others. Rajni was to come into office that day which added to my enthusiasm. A mail from AM awaited us in our inboxes. AM had sent a schedule for the 1–1 meetings and the dates when he expected the final ratings to be forwarded to the HR.

Subbu had a scorn on his face as I approached my desk. I smiled at Subbu before taking my seat and logging on.

Parag and Bhau walked in a few minutes later.

～

I locked my computer getting ready to go to the cafeteria for breakfast. Then I called up Rajni and informed her that we were going down to the cafeteria. Rajni had wanted to join us for breakfast. Her parents were away visiting relatives and, hence, she was free to have her breakfast at office for the whole week.

I collected a plate of bread–omelette for myself and two buttered toasts for Rajni before taking the seat next to Parag and others. Subbu picked one of the toasts I had brought for Rajni and started nibbling on it. I menacingly stared at Subbu.

'Don't stare at me, I am doing you a favour by helping Rajni stay thin,' said Subbu innocently.

Everyone around the table laughed. Rajni started eating the other piece of toast that was still there on the plate.

'Did you get an invite for a 1–1?' I asked to no one in particular.

'Yes, AM has sent the schedule to everyone in his team,' replied Parag.

Rajni was still nibbling at her toast. Subbu had finished eating his and was now eyeing my plate for a share of the bread–omelette.

'I don't think there is much to be expected from the appraisals. I just hate them!' added Bhau.

'I think we are so lucky to have such a nice manager,' added Rajni between nibbling at her toast.

Subbu looked at Rajni but thankfully did not share his views about beautiful girls and their managers.

We spent the rest of the breakfast talking about the appraisals and the 1–1 meetings.

After breakfast we trooped into the conference room to view the first scene. Bhau and Parag, our strongest critics, seemed to love the end result. I had put in our company logo on a white background to follow the initial scene. The orange logo stood out against the white and the additional word 'presents' in dark blue at the bottom.

Egged on by the results of the first scene, we decided to extend our meeting in the conference room in order to decide the way ahead for the movie.

～

I replayed the first scene in front of Rajni, Parag, Nidhi, Bhau and Subbu, all sitting around the conference table.

There were a few suggestions about the changes needed. Rajni wanted the scene that showed the toilet removed from the movie but we finally decided to let it stay though I agreed to shorten it a little.

Once everyone was satisfied, I explained my plan for the next scene. We finally left the conference room having decided that we would shoot the next scene early next day. Rajni's participation in the movie making provided the missing link that we had been looking for. She formed an effective bridge between us and Nidhi, helping us communicate with her without the fear of hurting her feelings.

~

That afternoon Rajni joined us for lunch. I was both pleased and pained to see her put in a genuine effort to involve herself in a conversation with others. She and Parag seemed to get along comfortably though I could sense some animosity between her and Subbu, but I was sure it would resolve itself once they got to know each other better.

Nidhi sat at the corner opposite Rajni. The movie had provided Rajni with an excuse to eat lunch and spend more time with me. It also saved her from having to provide excuses to Payal and Ashish for not joining them at their table for lunch.

~

That evening we shared the starting scene with Aman. He looked pleased with the way it had come out.

~

We assembled near the peepul tree close to my house. It was a huge tree that grew at the intersection of three roads. A cement platform had been built around it, which was used by people to place statues and other holy artefacts that they no longer wanted in their house. It had an air of sacredness to it.

The tree served the purpose for the scene as it was dense and stood against a backdrop of the rising sun.

Nidhi looked beautiful that morning. There was a hint of make-up on her face. She was wearing a pretty dress.

Rajni had done her job, and done it well.

Bhau rolled the camera as the sun began to rise.

Nidhi stood on the elevated platform around the tree awaiting Parag's signal to begin the shooting. The birds chirping overhead as they flew out of their nests in anticipation of the first meal of the day, provided a beautiful backdrop to the scene. The shooting started. Nidhi walked across the platform towards the camera speaking her lines.

'Nourishment and support are essential for a sapling to grow into a big and strong tree,' said Nidhi looking straight into the camera.

'Excellent!' shouted Subbu.

Subbu had taken the role of a spectator and critic since the time his camera responsibilities had been taken over by Bhau. He constantly shouted out expert comments to help us keep our spirits alive.

Bhau rewound the scene to see how it looked on the camera screen and was not very happy with the end results. He had wanted to bring in the sun and the myriad, vibrant colours of the sky into the scene.

We decided to re-shoot.

We had to shoot the same scene about four times before Bhau was satisfied.

Once we completed shooting we drove towards the office.

~

There was a lot of coding to be done and we were very busy catching up on the work. I made a futile attempt to fill up the column listing my objectives but could not make much progress and finally gave up.

That afternoon Rajni and Nidhi joined us for lunch again. I explained my idea for the next scene to the group over lunch. There was little else that occupied our conversation those days.

Everyone around the table broke down in splits of laughter when they heard my idea for the next scene. However, there was a problem, 'But where will we get the costumes from?' Parag suddenly interjected. Until now there had been no talk of dresses or clothes.

There was silence around the table when Nidhi finally spoke up, 'I think I can manage that. One of my father's friends is a costume designer and he may be able to help us out.'

We cancelled the movie meeting that evening and drove to Nidhi's uncle's shop. And although the stuff there did not quite fit the bill, we found something close to what we wanted.

It was late at night when I finally reached home.

Dad was invariably forced to make alternate arrangements for his transport as the movie, along with the coding and appraisal, took away most of my time.

~

The next day we assembled around the training room to shoot the scene for which we had collected the costumes. Subbu, Parag and Bhau, dressed like heroes from cowboy movies, were ready for the shoot. They were shown entering the training room and finally coming out dressed in coats and ties burdened with loads of books. The scene was to play against the score from *The Good, the Bad and the Ugly*.

As days passed our confidence in the film grew and so did our skills behind and in front of the camera. Ideas continued to flow and the movie was adding up into what we had initially wanted to achieve.

~

However, we had fallen behind on our delivery schedules for the codes. AM had been very annoyed with our lack of commitment to the pending components. Then AM and Aman sorted things between themselves. While Aman worked with us on the movie, AM ensured that we still concentrated on the coding; that was our foremost responsibility.

There seemed to be an invisible wall between the two of them. Initially I had thought it was probably just my imagination, but later, when I spoke to Subbu, I realized that everyone had noticed it.

Both Aman and AM abided by this invisible wall, never crossing it. AM had decided on his areas of concern, while Aman seemed to have taken up what was left.

We were like the proverbial ropes that kept getting pulled in two opposite directions.

So while we had a timeline for the movie, AM had also set a deadline for the self reviews at the Thursday meeting.

He wanted us to complete the self reviews with the ratings by the weekend, which practically left us just one day to complete things at our end.

My 1–1 was scheduled for the coming Tuesday.

~

Satisfied with the progress we had made with the movie, we decided to take a break on Friday. We had to complete our self appraisals and did not want to fall back on the schedule AM had set for us.

After much consideration I had decided to rate myself '3' in most of the objectives. The ratings started with '5' as the lowest and ended at '1', the highest possible rating. A rating of '3' implied that the person was just able to scrape through and achieved what was expected from him. It also implied that the employee was an average performer.

The biggest chunk of company employees fitted into '3'.

I knew I would be lucky to scrape through with average ratings from AM.

~

Tuesday was upon us faster than we anticipated.

I got into office that morning dreading how the 1-1 session with AM was going to be. The thoughts from the previous sessions kept creeping back into my mind, keeping me on tenterhooks.

I wondered if Aman would join us this time.

Then I sat glued to my seat the entire morning trying to come up with strategies to defend myself. I ate little during breakfast or lunch. Rajni was the only one concerned at my lack of appetite while others continued making fun about my fear.

Bhau was first to have his 1-1 with AM and he shared his experience with us after the session. He was not terribly disappointed with the way things had gone. AM had given him a '2' for most of his objectives and a '1' for delivery. Bhau had also mentioned that Aman was sitting with AM in the meeting. It was Aman who had wanted AM to give Bhau an overall rating of '1' but AM had persisted with his views. Aman had also hinted during the meeting that AM should make a case for Bhau's promotion but AM had promised little. However, as a rule the rating of '2' was an above average rating and that meant that Bhau would get a good hike this time.

I felt a short-lived relief after listening to Bhau's experience. But soon that too gave way to my own concerns

I walked into Austin, fearing the worst. I had remembered to pick up my diary this time and had also made note of things that I wanted to highlight about my performance. I excused myself as I entered Austin.

Aman was sitting by AM's side but was not taking any notes this time.

'Welcome Anup! How are you feeling today?' Aman said rather amicably.

AM lifted his eyes from the sheets, which I supposed were my objectives and self rating, to look at me.

'We are really pleased with the improvement you have shown this time. I think you really deserve a big pat on your back,' added Aman smiling.

AM had a neutral look on his face. I sat silently smiling at Aman and AM, praying that nothing untoward would happen.

'Anup, let us start going through your objectives one by one,' AM spoke for the first time since the meeting began.

'Self Management . . .' he said, reading out the points I had written against my first objective. It was few minutes before he finished reading the points I had filled in and spoke to me 'I think you deserve a two here,' AM said smiling for the first time since the meeting had started. I was surprised at AM's suggestion. I wondered if I had heard him right.

'Pardon me?' I said wanting to confirm what I had heard.

AM chuckled before adding, 'Don't look surprised, I am really happy with the way things have developed during the last few weeks since our first 1-1 meeting. I want to rate you a "2" because of your positive attitude and hard work.'

I was relieved by the way things had started at the meeting. I had not expected a '2' for any of my objectives.

AM ran through the other objectives one by one.

'Work Process and Results, I think you still need to improve here. Your deliverables have left a little too much wanting. I don't think you deserve more than a "4" here.' I felt my heart suddenly sink. A rating of '4' meant that I was below average. If an employee got an overall rating of '4' he invariably ended up being pulled up by the HR and was placed under observation. A rating of '5' was even worse and could mean only one thing—being asked to leave the organization. There were very few employees who ever got a '5'. The worst performers were rated '4'. Both '4' and '5' meant that the employee did not get any hikes for the year.

My heart skipped a beat as we moved on to the next objective.

'Teamwork, I think you deserve a "3" there,' said AM before moving on.

AM quickly ran through the other objectives 'Innovation and Change', 'Development', 'Communication', 'Customer Service' before summarizing my overall rating.

'I think we will settle for an overall rating of "3" this time but you need to do really well to maintain it for the next year.

I think you have the potential for a "2" but don't have the will power to strive for it,' added AM as he summarized my appraisal for me.

I sighed with relief as the meeting drew to a close—it had gone much better than what I had hoped for!

I rushed to Subbu's seat and shared with him everything that had transpired in the meeting. Subbu looked at me disdainfully before adding, 'You must be the first employee to be so happy about a "3" rating.' What Subbu had said was true but at that stage the worst was over and I cared little for what Subbu or anyone else thought.

~

Nidhi had called in sick, which meant that there was little we could shoot that day. Rajni had agreed to stay back to help us with the movie. And that's when I got the chance to speak to her about my session.

She turned around thoughtfully and said, 'Anup I don't think you fit into the IT industry. I sometimes wonder if you should stop working and look for something more creative.'

I did not give much thought to what she had said then, but looking back I realize the profundity of her words.

'Let's go and check on Parag,' I suggested as we finished our tea. Rajini said she would join in later.

Parag seemed busy looking at the recordings when I entered the room. He was lost, looking at something on the screen. I looked up from Parag to the television screen. The screen was paused on a close-up of Nidhi's face. Then suddenly, realizing that some one had come into the conference room, he fidgeted with the remote trying to find the play button.

There was an uncomfortable silence between us. When Rajni walked in a few seconds later, Parag and I were still struggling to find things to say. I smiled at Parag trying to ignore what had passed before Rajni had entered.

'Hey rewind the movie,' I added helpfully trying to release the tension.

'Yes, please do, I want to see it from the start,' said Rajni taking a seat next to me. Parag rewound the movie before playing it on again.

'Hold it there!' I shouted rushing to take the remote from Parag. I hit the pause button to pause the movie on the frame that showed a shot of Nidhi's face. It was the very same frame which Parag had been looking at when I had come in.

I stood there watching and admiring Nidhi's face on the screen. There was an innocence that could disarm any one. The face spoke words without moving, it conveyed trust and it conveyed determination, resolution and integrity. It was not the face that struck me then . . . But it was the complete movie that was staring back at me. I realized I had found what I had been looking for. I admired the frame for a few seconds more before looking back at Parag and Rajni. They were both confused with my reaction.

'Hey listen to this,' I said excited about my plan, before adding 'We will use this frame against a white background for the ending. We will fade out Nidhi's face as the words: We build relationships . . . Products just happen, appear on the screen,' I could see the entire scene play out in front of my eyes. I could feel the impact that the scene would have on the crowd.

I stood there basking in the satisfaction of having found the final scene for our movie . . . I knew I had found the 'perfect scene'.

15

NIDHI

A story unfinished, hidden in seams of despair
A music note crying out into the realms of nowhere
An open book with empty pages staring into our faces
. . . was all that had been left to the end.
Neither could time ease the pain, nor would a million words
suffice.
What happened then had been god's will, a roll of dice, a
twist in tail, the last stone, that none of us could change.

~

Parag confided in me that evening after Rajni had left. We had walked down for a smoke when Parag opened up without any initiation from my side. I looked at the dark sky and heard his words but their meaning was lost on me. I stood, admiring the darkness, searching for the stars. I could not see the moon. It was too bright to be a moonless night. The moon was probably hidden behind the clouds, waiting for the opportune moment to make an appearance. I held on to the railing that ran around our office building, thinking of the first time Rajni and I had

exchanged the three wonderful words. The feeling I had
then had still not gone away . . .

I had been waiting for days to say those words to Rajni.
It seemed as if I had been waiting forever to hold her
tightly in my arms, to tell her the way I felt about her . . .

We had been talking for a few minutes on the phone
everyday, but were yet to disclose our feelings for each
other. And though no words were needed to convey what
I felt, I longed to speak them out.

~

A gust of wind hit me on my face. It felt good to feel the
breeze through my hair and shirt.

'Anup, are you listening to me?' asked Parag desperately.

'I need a beer,' I replied. 'And I will call home and let
my parents know that I will be staying at your place. We
can take the car to your flat and probably buy a few bottles
of beer on the way.'

'Okay,' Parag agreed, probably realizing that I was far
away.

Then he asked, 'But what about Subbu and Bhau? I
don't want them to come. I want to talk to you first.'

We walked up the flight of stairs, not wanting to take
the lift, while trying to come up with an excuse for Subbu
and Bhau.

~

It had been the day before our first Valentine's Day
together. I wanted to gift something special to Rajni,
something that would convey my feelings, something that
Rajni would cherish for the rest of her life. I felt a little
foolish being, flooded with emotions that the soppy,

romantic songs from the radio and the advertisement hoardings made me feel. Earlier, it had meant little more than gimmickry by card companies, and yet, today I was a part of it all.

I had spent hours earlier in the day trying to pick up an e-card for Rajni and had finally settled for a simple card with a basket of white roses that surrounded a single red rose. I had filled in my feelings before forwarding it to Rajni.

Then she sent me our first SMS that night: Happy Valentine's Day!

I checked the clock by my bedside: 12.10 a.m. it read.

'Same to you ... Miss you!' I replied immediately unable to wait.

We had exchanged a few more SMSs before I found the courage and typed, 'Can I call you now?' It was nearly 1.00 a.m.

I waited anxiously for a reply from Rajni. She gave me a missed call instead of replying. Taking it as a sign of consent, I immediately dialled her number.

'Love you Anup,' Rajni had answered at the first ring, trying to keep her voice as low as possible. She did not want to wake up her sister who was sleeping in the same room.

'Love you too dear,' I had blurted out, lacking better words to summarize my feelings. We had talked for a few more minutes that night. And till date those words still have the same effect on me, every time Rajni utters them.

~

We reached our desks to find Subbu already packing his things for the day. 'I am feeling very sleepy. I am leaving now. See you guys tomorrow!' he blurted as he switched off his computer and started to leave.

'Wait!' Bhau interjected, 'Let me come along, even I am finding it difficult to concentrate today.'

Parag and I put in a feeble attempt to try and stop them but to our relief both of them left a few minutes later.

After about fifteen minutes Parag and I too decided to call it a day. And before long we had logged off our machines and were heading towards the car park.

We picked up a few bottles of our favourite beer and got our dinner packed from Shiva's before heading towards Parag's flat.

~

I opened the bottle of beer filling up the glasses. Subconsciously, I was trying to delay what I knew would soon be coming.

'Anup, I think I am beginning to like Nidhi,' Parag blurted out before taking a large gulp from his glass.

I opened the pack of peanuts and emptied them into the plate.

'Do you have some onions and tomatoes,' I asked trying to steer away from the conversation. Then I stood up and walked to the kitchen to help myself with the onions and tomatoes. I had stayed over at Parag's flat a few times and knew where to find them. Having found what I was looking for, I started to peel the onions. Parag followed me into the kitchen a few minutes later.

The image I had built of Parag in my mind was of strong and mature man who was always at hand to solve my troubles and provide suggestions. Of a person who put me at ease. And of someone who was always calm and worried little about what life had to throw at him.

Now I was finding it hard to exchange places with him.

~

Parag's statement hung loosely between us like a wet curtain. I finished cutting half the onion before I replied directly to Parag's question for the first time that evening.

'Pooja?' I asked looking directly at Parag. Pooja was Parag's fiancée to be.

'She has called me a few times this week. Pooja thinks that there is something that has been troubling me and I am hiding it from her. I have stopped answering her calls since yesterday. I am afraid that she will find out,' Parag replied morosely.

I walked out to the living room to collect my glass. I emptied and refilled it before carrying the bottle and the glass back into the kitchen.

'Your glass,' I said stretching out the hand that held the bottle towards Parag. 'Have you spoken to Nidhi about your feelings?'

'No,' he replied as we walked back from the kitchen with the cut tomatoes and onions.

I mixed the peanuts with the tomatoes and onions before adding some salt and pepper.

'Parag, I don't know what to tell you, but it looks like you are in a big mess,' I said. 'Just think of how your parents will react to this?'

'I don't know.'

I could see the desperation in his eyes.

'Have you spoken to anyone else? . . . Subbu?' Subbu

according to me was the best person to advice during such situations.

'I am not worried about my parents. I am worried about Pooja. She will be shattered if she hears this. I don't know what I am going to do,' said Parag. I could see he was close to breaking down into tears.

'I can imagine how Pooja would react. I know from experience.' It had never been really bad between Rajni and me but I knew how possessive or jealous girls could sometimes get. And in this case I thought Parag was at fault.

We sat there thinking for a long time as we finished what was left of our drinks. Parag was looking a little relieved after having shared his secret with me. Then suddenly his phone rang, breaking the silence that had set in between us. Parag answered the phone before walking out to the balcony.

I switched on the television and opened the last bottle of beer to refill our glasses. I wondered about Parag's troubles as I browsed through the channels. I remembered how close I had been once to falling in love with Nidhi. I wondered how Rajni would have reacted then.

It was thirty minutes before Parag finally returned.

'Pooja?' I asked, looking up at him expectantly.

Parag hesitated before replying.

'No, Nidhi.'

~

Parag sat down facing me across the small table. I tried to concentrate on the television trying to hide my displeasure. We continued to watch the bollywood song and dance without exchanging words. I kept mum, not wanting to share my true feelings.

'You are serious about Nidhi, aren't you?' I asked in a sarcastic tone. It felt foolish to ask such a question of your friend. Parag looked across at me; his eyes told me what a million words could not. At that moment I knew Parag was deep in love with Nidhi.

I did not blame Parag. It was hard to avoid falling in love with a girl like Nidhi.

Nidhi was everything that a man could desire in a wife. The more time you spent with Nidhi the harder it was to stay away from her. The other problem that I guessed was the distance between Pooja and Parag. I knew what distance could do to the strongest of relationships. Parag and Pooja would have been engaged by now if only Pooja's grandmother had not passed away. The engagement ceremony had been delayed by six months because of the untimely demise.

Parag and Pooja were to be engaged a month from today. I doubted if the engagement would happen given the developments. We quietly ate our dinner before hitting the bed.

I had slept fitfully that night troubled by Parag's story and the beer that left me wanting to empty my bladder at regular intervals.

We did not talk about the subject again.

~

The next morning in office I was unable to contain Parag's secret and had shared what I had learnt with Rajni and Subbu. Rajni was furious with Parag. She thought that Parag had acted foolishly and irresponsibly. I think Rajni would have killed Parag if he had made the mistake of coming in front of her.

'Goddamn it! He is going to get engaged next month. Imagine the plight of that poor girl!' she blurted out seething with anger.

I could not speak any further about this subject with Rajni. Subbu on the other hand had listened calmly and even seemed amused with what I had to say.

'You don't have a choice! You just fall in love. It happens.' He pouted wisdom and then slowly and thoughtfully added, 'It is better to spoil one life instead of two.'

I wondered if it was ever going to be as simple as that.

16

THE FINAL CUT

It was 11.30 p.m. on Sunday night.

This was the last weekend before the big event where the films by the various aspirants were to be showcased. It also was our last chance at making any additions or changes to the movie. However, we were still a few hours away from finishing the movie. Aman had visited us in the evening at the studio and had been watching us work. He had finally called it a day and was getting ready to leave for home because he had a very important meeting early next morning with the head of the organization and a few clients which he could not afford to miss. But before he went, he had let us know that we could come in late to office the next morning.

Parag and I had walked Aman down before heading out to look for dinner. We scoured the entire area around the studio for a liquor store that would sell us beer. Food was not a big problem as there were still some small restaurants that were open, but what we wanted most on a night like this was beer. We finally returned to the studio with two bottles of beer and a lot of greasy food.

The hungry group, which included the two of us, dug into the food without caring much for appearance or taste. We savoured the two bottles of beer like it was the elixir of life. Then we cleaned up the table before getting back to work inside the editing room.

~

Two weeks ago . . .

We sat in the conference room watching the reruns from the movie.

'You have improved tremendously from when we started,' I commented, looking towards Nidhi who was sitting across the table while Parag was perched on the ledge next to where she sat. Subbu was standing in front of the white marker board in the opposite corner. Bhau sat on the seat closest to the television, watching the movie intently.

'I think this scene needs to be shot again,' Bhau said, commenting on the scene we had shot an hour ago. He was our biggest critic and had helped us cut and trim the movie into its current shape.

There were some scenes in the movie where Nidhi had looked so captivating that it was hard to peel ones eyes away from the screen.

~

Over the four weeks that we had been involved in shooting the film, we had spent so much time together that we now understood each other well.

'There is something amiss with the movie, it still lacks the professional touch,' commented Parag to no one in particular.

Then Aman entered the conference room, cutting Parag short. He asked for it to be replayed. Subbu hit the rewind button. We had already watched the movie a few hundred times. Aman had loved the movie, but agreed with Parag that there was still something amiss.

~

During our discussion in the conference room I had noticed Parag and Nidhi exchange glances a few times. It was a little hard for me to accept the chemistry between them. I had initially begun to concentrate on the film and tried to ignore them. However, soon my inquisitiveness had got the better of me and I had followed Parag when he left the conference room to get himself a tea.

'Have you told Nidhi about Pooja?' I queried catching up with Parag as we neared the coffee machine.

Parag seemed to be surprised. I wondered what life had in store for these two. Parag was still to tell Nidhi about Pooja. He also knew it had to be sooner than later. There were also Parag's parents who needed to be convinced. We could only guess as to how Nidhi's parents would react to the news.

~

'I think I know what we need,' said Aman, rushing over to our desks the next day. Bhau, Subbu, Parag and I were busy catching up on our coding. We looked up, surprised by the sudden interruption.

'What we need is a professional editor and a day or two at a studio,' added Aman, after making sure he had our attention. 'The other group that is working on the movie has hired a professional editor and I don't see any reason why we should also not do the same.'

'But it is going to cost us money,' I retorted, half annoyed at the sudden interruption Aman had caused.

'Oh, don't worry. I've got friends and will be able to work out a deal. The company has agreed to allot Rs 15,000 to each group working on the movie. So the budget should not be a problem any longer.' Aman looked animated as he spoke.

~

There was little more than a week before the grand event where the movie was to be showcased.

The code we were working on had to be delivered a week after the event. We were spending more time on the movie, hoping that we would be able to catch up with the coding in the week between the event and the delivery date. We were blissfully unaware that the next two weeks in question would change our lives forever!

~

It was Friday; I was very excited about the way things had turned out with the movie.

We had visited the studio and talked things out with the in charge there. A slot had been booked at the studio for our use over the weekend.

~

The interviews I had conducted with Aman had gone surprisingly well. Of the five candidates that I had interviewed we had selected three.

~

Rajni had loved the movie we were shooting and could not stop raving about the script. I had noticed that Payal and Ashish were annoyed with the way Rajni was reacting. They got angry every time she started talking about me or the movie. They were probably shocked at the sudden transformation in their friend.

I finished my coding and joined Rajni for a cup of tea. She was leaving early that day as she had some shopping to do for her sister's birthday. I walked back to my seat to check on the others after my walk with Rajni. I noticed Bhau and Subbu coding at their desks.

'Where is Parag?' I asked. He was not at his seat. Things had changed between Parag and me in the last few days. I had now transformed into Parag's advisor and guide. Parag and I had finally swapped places.

'He must be in the conference room with Nidhi,' said Subbu carelessly, not bothering to look away from his computer. Since I had lumbered all day with my modules, the last thing I wanted to do now was to get back to my desk and work on the modules again. I decided to join Parag and Nidhi in the conference room.

Nidhi and Parag were caught by surprise when I opened the door to the conference room. The television had been switched off and the video camera was no where in sight. I realized that they had not been working on the movie. I felt rather uncomfortable having intruded their discussion. I could make out that Nidhi had been crying. Not wanting to increase their discomfort I excused myself before starting to leave.

'Come in Anup, you don't have to leave,' said Nidhi trying to hide the fact that she had been crying.

'Umm . . . no, I have to catch up on the coding,' I

replied trying to sound casual. I wanted to leave the conference room as quickly as possible.

'Please come in Anup,' said Parag. Nidhi nodded at me, this time she did not try to hide her tears. I quickly closed the door behind me before taking to the seat next to Parag. I did not want to put Parag and Nidhi in a spot. I also did not want others to learn about what was happening inside the conference room.

'Anup, why don't you explain it to him,' said Nidhi with tears gushing down her face.

I looked helplessly at Parag. Parag seemed to sink deeper into the chair.

'Anup, please tell him that it would never work,' Nidhi turned around and rushed out of the conference room unable to control her emotions.

I looked at Parag, trying to understand what had just happened: Parag had finally found the courage to speak to Nidhi about Pooja. His parents had called him wanting him to come home in a few weeks' time to make preparations for the engagement. Parag, realizing that he had very little time left, had broken the news to Nidhi.

Nidhi had been shocked.

She was silent for a while before erupting in fury. She had shouted at Parag and then had broken down in tears before she made the decision for both herself and Parag. When I had come in, Nidhi had been trying to convince Parag that their relationship had no future any longer. She was trying to tell Parag that he needed to go ahead with the engagement to Pooja and not anger his family by going against them.

Parag was not convinced with Nidhi's line of thought and had tried to argue against it.

Nidhi had replied, 'Parag I can't be the reason for someone's pain. Just imagine what Pooja would feel when she learns about our relationship. I cannot imagine myself going through my life wondering how I stole someone else's husband. I can't live someone else's dreams!'

That had been the last we saw of Nidhi that day. We later learnt that she had rushed out of the office without having provided an explanation to anyone. Parag tried Nidhi's mobile number a few times before finally giving up in exasperation.

We left office late that night deciding to meet at the studio next day. I offered to drop Parag at his flat and also told him that he could give the studio a miss the next day, if he wanted to.

Parag rejected both my suggestions. He said he would feel much better spending time at the studio than sitting alone and rueing his fate.

~

The next day we drove to Noida using the directions Aman had provided us. He was waiting for us at the gate.

The houses in the area looked opulent. In between these beautiful houses, where the richest people in Delhi lived, was the studio. It was well hidden from the outside world. Nothing about the house except for the number told you that it was the answer to your search for a studio.

As we entered the house, we were hit by the buzz of activity that was going on inside. There were multiple editing rooms for all the budding directors. The rooms were filled with up-to-date gizmo. Aman had already worked out a deal through his contacts. We were directly ushered into the editing room where a technician was sitting in front of the computer waiting for us to arrive before he could start work on our movie.

We worked round the clock with the technician helping us put our thoughts to screen. Bhau had made us redo most of the scenes a few hundred times before he was happy. For us, therefore, the final product from all our efforts was probably nothing short of a masterpiece!

Parag had gone missing at times only to return looking even sadder. My guess was that he was trying to call Nidhi, who was still refusing to answer his calls. I did not know what to tell Subbu and Bhau when they looked questioningly at me every time Parag walked out.

Nidhi finally answered Parag's call around evening. They spoke for an hour. Parag returned with a smile on his face. He even acted his normal self for the next few minutes before going back to being glum. We finally called it a day, late on Saturday night, agreeing to regroup at the studio early next morning. We just had one more day to get the movie ready for the event!

17

THE ROLL OF THE DICE

Aman called us up at 6.00 a.m. on Monday morning. We had stayed overnight at the studio working on the movie.

'Aman, most of the work is done. The movie is nearly ready. All we need to do is put in the acknowledgements and the credits at the end. We will leave once that is done,' I said, excited with the way the film had turned out.

'Hey, don't worry about it. Just go home and get some sleep. I will take care of the rest. I need to be there when boss comes over for a sneak preview of the movies,' Aman replied.

After much convincing, I reluctantly agreed to leave, still unsure if we should not wait to complete the last bits. I went back and told the others what Aman had suggested. They also did not want to move till the movie was complete, and so we decided to stay on.

We finally finished the work around eight in the morning. The movie ended with frames of funny incidents that we had shot, alongside the acknowledgements and the credits. The credits and acknowledgements followed a few seconds after the perfect scene . . . the profile of Nidhi's face on a white background that slowly faded out as the company tag line and logo made its appearance in orange against a black background.

'We build relationships, products just happen'

It looked wonderful. We requested the technician to cut us a few copies of the movie, not wanting to wait until the next day before we could give others a sneak preview.

~

We reached home around 9.00 a.m. and took a short nap before heading to the office that afternoon. Mom and Dad had already seen the movie a few hundred times.

That evening, Subbu, Parag, Bhau, Nidhi, Rajni, Payal and I sat in the conference room watching it and appreciating our handiwork. Rajni was all praises. She walked over to me and whispered into my ears, 'I knew it would turn out this good. After all, my Anup has worked on it.' I loved the way Rajni had said that. I loved the pride and sense of ownership that her voice had conveyed. We had been loaded with praises from everyone who had seen the movie, but, for me, Rajni's view had mattered the most and even though she agreed that she loved it, I could sense a slight envy when she spoke about the 'perfect scene'.

We were happy with the way things had turned out. Even Bhau, our strongest critic was full of praises. Aman called us that evening to confirm that our movie had been selected to be showcased. He added that there were a few bits that needed to be changed but assured us that nothing important had been removed. The changes made were minor. He even wanted to show us the final cut before the event, but we agreed that we were happy to abide by his decision.

We happily worked on the coding, knowing well that the first of our two tasks was a success.

Subbu suggested that we should go to Shiva's and celebrate, but Bhau overruled him since there was a lot of work that needed to be completed.

~

There was another event unfolding behind our backs, unknown to us.

On Sunday night I had shared with Subbu what had transpired between Parag and Nidhi. We had gone down for a smoke while the others were busy making the final changes to the movie or catching a few winks. Unable to contain my sympathy for Parag, I had opened up to Subbu.

'Fools,' was all that Subbu had said in response before we headed back to the studio to join others.

In the following days he spoke little about Parag and Nidhi, so I assumed that he had forgotten all about it.

Then a few days later, Parag rushed to Subbu's desk and thanked him profusely for all that he had done. I realized that something had happened behind the scenes which I had completely missed. Parag told us that he had informed his parents about Nidhi and his relationship. Initially, they had been furious but after realizing that Parag could not be shaken from his decision, they had slammed the phone down suggesting that he could do whatever he thought was best. Parag had then broken the news to Pooja, who broke down before berating him.

Parag seemed reasonably happy with the way things had turned out. He was sure that things would return to normal with time. And, most importantly, he now had Nidhi by his side.

18

THE EVENT

It was D-Day. We reached the venue early and took our seats. Rajni, Payal and Nidhi were sitting in the same row as us: Parag, Subbu, Bhau and me.

The event began with introductions and presentations about the achievements of the company. We anxiously awaited the filming session. Each time the anchor took to stage with the mike to announce the next item on the agenda, we hoped that it was going to be our movie.

The head of the organization walked up to the stage to make his presentation. He ran us through the various slides and events that had been defining moments for the company in the last five years. He finally concluded, 'Let us all take some time to watch a wonderful movie that was made by your friends. I am sure you will all love it as much as I did.'

He signalled for the movie to start. The hall darkened and the movie began to play. I could see Rajni's eyes glistening with tears. I looked around watching the eager faces, unable to peel their eyes from the screen. I waited impatiently for their reactions, for the time when we would be drowned in praises.

When the last part began, the entire hall went silent. The laughter brought on from the previous scenes faded out as Nidhi's face filled up the screen. It slowly gave way to admiration. Nidhi smiled on screen before fading out and being replaced by the company's logo and mission statement.

I was mesmerized looking at the tears flowing out of Rajni's eyes. She made little attempt to hide or wipe them away. I knew what to expect next. I had seen the movie enough to know it by heart. I knew that the funny scenes accompanied with the acknowledgements and credits would soon follow. As the movie ended, the room broke into a huge applause.

I heard Subbu shouting into my ears, 'Hey, none of our names are there! The last bit with the acknowledgements and credits has been cut off!' said Subbu. He sounded extremely annoyed. We looked around to the spot where Aman was sitting. We could not wait to ask him why he had cut the part with our names on it.

The head of the organization took to the stage amid all the applause that filled the hall. He waited for the noise to ebb out before starting to speak. 'I think we should take time to appreciate the efforts that have gone into this movie. I am proud to call up on the stage the man who has done wonders in the short time he has been with us. He is a person who has been an inspiration for people around and has also constantly delivered against all odds. I call up on the stage the man who made this movie possible. Mr Aman Sharma!'

The room again broke into a huge applause.

Rajni gave me a quizzical look.

I felt a pain rise from deep within my heart. My throat

went dry, and I needed a drink badly. I stood up and left the auditorium, not wanting to see the rest of the show. As I walked out of the door into the open, a cold draft of fresh air hit me, but the pain in my heart continued to grow.

I walked away from the hall into the dark, not knowing where I was heading. I stopped to look up at the clear sky. The twinkling stars seemed to be smiling at me. I must have stood there for a long time watching the stars, deeply immersed in my thoughts. Then I felt a hand on my shoulders and turned around hoping that whoever it was would not notice the tears in my eyes. We had given everything we had to the movie and now to watch someone walk away with the credit was nothing short of a death blow.

Rajni stood behind me. She was looking into my eyes. I could hardly control myself as the pain rose through me and finally engulfed me. She moved in closer and put her arms around me. I broke down into sobs, letting my head fall on her shoulder.

I cried like a baby.

I cried like there was no tomorrow.

I could smell the sweet perfume of Rajni's hair. I could feel her heart beating against my chest. As her warmth filled me my pain eased. At that moment I knew I loved Rajni more than anything in this world. I knew that I could die for her and I realized then that Rajni had always been mine.

The pain in my chest eased, and my sobbing petered down, but I did not want to move my head from her shoulders. There was warmth and there was such comfort in that embrace that I did not want to lose it.

Rajni and I stood under the night sky holding each other unaware of time and the world that surrounded us. I slowly raised my head to look into Rajni's face. I was looking at the most beautiful face in the world. Rajni gasped, I could feel her heart beat quicken. I could feel the warmth that rose to her face like a blush. Her eyes were shut but she had sensed that I was looking at her closely. She looked up at me, tilting her head towards my face. I slowly moved my face closer to hers, feeling the warmth of her breath, before we kissed. We kissed for the first time ever, forgetting about everything around us. We kissed because in that moment nothing had mattered more than having each other.

~

We walked towards my car hand in hand and drove away from the auditorium. We drove away from AM, Aman and KK. We drove away from Subbu, Parag and Bhau. We drove because we needed no one else. I dropped Rajni at her place before heading back home. I was rather pleased with the way the day had turned out. I had something that was worth much more than the movie. I had something that was worth more than any credit that credit pinchers like Aman could garner.

I had something that was mine . . . something that no one could take away or steal from me.

In Rajni, I had love.

19

A TWIST IN THE TAIL

I slept through the weekend catching up on much-needed sleep. Rajni had called me twice over the weekend to confirm if everything was all right.

I loved the attention Rajni was showering on me.

Through the day my thoughts kept wandering back to the night of celebration and I had mixed feelings about the evening—the disappointment around the movie, the happiness after the brief but most romantic encounter with Rajni added to my confusion. The excitement was over and there was definite a sense of loss. I wanted to sort out my feelings but it felt as if Monday morning was upon me much sooner than I had anticipated. I dropped Dad at his office before driving along at a leisurely pace to my office.

Having to do something that you dislike is the hardest part of life. The events from Friday had left me deflated and a feeling of helplessness had crept into my heart. It was ironical that one day I was on my way to achieving everything I had set out to achieve and the very next day I stood defeated in a battle that I had never fought. I was reduced to nothing more than a mere spectator watching someone else walk away with my trophy.

Subbu's words kept ringing in my ears, 'You know the problem with you, Anup, is that you trust people too easily.' I had learnt an important lesson that weekend, one that I would never forget.

An organization is nothing but the people who work in it. It is the people like Aman, AM and KK, who are our immediate superiors that govern our impressions of the company. So, a company can be good if your manager is good and bad if the manager is incompetent or inordinately demanding. From the toad's view that I had about our organization, things looked rather bleak. I had Aman and AM to make up my workday with KK filling in when he could.

Looking back, I always end up wondering if there was a way that things could have turned out differently.

~

I sank into the chair at my desk and logged on to my computer.

It was still pretty early in the morning and people had just started trickling into office. I browsed through my emails before logging on to the mainframe to start work on the module I was writing. I braced myself for a busy week ahead. There were a lot of things to catch up on since we had neglected the components because of the movie work.

'Hi, good morning,' said Subbu as he took his seat. Parag and Bhau also walked in a little while later.

'Let's go down for a bite,' suggested Parag. We all walked towards the steps. I followed Bhau and the others taking the shorter route.

Friday had changed things between Rajni and me. If

the situation with Ashish had started the change in Rajni then the events from Friday had completed the transformation. I no longer needed to steal glances at Rajni. I did not crave for constant emails or phone calls from her. I no longer craved for proofs of her love. We were closer to each other than we ever were. Of course, the fact that Rajni had brought our relationship into the open had also helped.

We were all silent over breakfast. No one wanted to talk about the movie.

'I am going to kill him!' said Subbu, finally breaking the silence.

Parag smiled ruefully before adding, 'Wish we could have done that.'

'I think we should talk to him and ask for an explanation. He owes us that much after all that has happened,' I suggested not wanting to utter Aman's name.

Bhau had a smirk on his face and kept silent through our conversation. I assumed that he was thinking of his chances at getting the promotion during this appraisal period. And so he obviously did not want to ruffle any feathers, knowing well that it would all be in vain, anyway. He would probably wait until the results on the annual appraisal were out before letting go of his feelings into the open. Bhau probably wanted the hike and the promotion more than any of us, not to mention the fact that he also deserved it the most.

After finishing breakfast, we headed back to our desks.

Bhau drowned himself into the green and black screen, while Subbu and I contemplated walking over to Aman and asking him for an explanation. Parag suggested that we send Aman an invitation to a meeting instead of confronting him directly.

I remembered that Aman had briefly appeared at his desk that morning before disappearing suddenly. He was gone before Subbu or I could decide on how to confront him.

~

Around 11.00 a.m., an email from AM appeared on the right hand corner of my screen. I opened the mail, thinking it had something to do with the code we had to deliver. The subject on the mail surprised me. I turned to look at Subbu. There was surprise written all over his face too.

'My last day in the organization,' said the subject.

Hi All,

This could come as a surprise to you but it has been in the pipeline for quite sometime. I have put in my papers and will be leaving this organization today. I have handed over all my responsibilities to Aman, and he will be taking over the team. I am sure you will meet all your future commitments in the same timely manner as we have done in the past.

Do feel free to get in touch with me if you need anything.

AM had provided his contact details at the end of the email just in case anyone wanted to contact him.

This surely would have been a cause for celebration on any other day, but not today.

We were still to recover from Friday.

We were too engrossed in problems of our own to be able to give much thought to AM. To be frank, neither of us was sure if the news about AM leaving was good or bad. After what Aman had done, it was hard to tell the difference between who was worse.

Parag had walked over to Subbu's seat, and I had joined them. We reread the mail together just to be sure.

'This is a surprise,' said Parag after having completed reading the mail the second time.

'I thought he would have stayed until the delivery was complete. It is very unlike of AM to leave at a time like this,' added Subbu.

'From what I have come to know of AM, I would have thought that he would have waited to add another feather to his cap before he left!' I contemplated loud enough for the others to hear.

'I agree,' added Parag.

We were engrossed in our little conversation when another email from AM popped up on Subbu's screen.

Subbu eagerly opened it

'I think he is trying to recall his previous email. Someone must have played a prank on AM,' said Subbu, smiling as we waited for the email to open.

'Just a small meeting,' said the subject.

The email was addressed to the four of us:

Hi guys,

I know I should have warned you earlier, but it is probably not too late yet. Can we meet at Shiva's, the shop down the road, today in the evening around 6.30 p.m.? I know you are all busy trying to meet your commitments, but I will not keep you long!'

We were more perplexed than before. If the first mail was surprising, the second was even more intriguing.

'What could he possibly want?' asked Subbu, turning to face me and Parag.

'I don't want to go,' said Bhau, standing up in his cubicle.

'Oh! You do read your emails,' quipped Parag with a smile.

Bhau glared back at Parag before adding, 'Are you guys going?'

'Imagine, of all the places, he wants to meet at Shiva's. If he wants to give us a farewell treat, he should have at least chosen a better place.'

'I don't think this is about a farewell dinner. AM is not a person who believes in such things. He probably just wants to remind us about our commitments,' said Subbu, laughing.

'He probably wants us to join him at the new organization,' added Bhau helpfully.

I wondered if that could be true.

I could understand if AM wanted to take Bhau along with him, but what about Subbu and me?

~

Nidhi, Rajni and Payal joined us for lunch. I had told Rajni about AM's resignation. From then on the only topic that everyone wanted to talk about was the resignation. We contemplated what the invitation from AM meant. What was more surprising was that there had been no signs of Aman after our little encounter this morning.

~

Rajni called me at my desk around 5.30 that evening. She was leaving with Payal for the day.

'Yes! I am fine, there is nothing wrong,' I replied for the hundredth time since Friday. Rajni was still far from convinced.

'I know it is hard, but you need to move on! It probably is for the best,' continued Rajni. She was playing the part of the counsellor to the hilt! Somehow she reminded me of my mother who sometimes carried on trying to placate me long after I had forgotten about the incident!

'I am still thinking about what AM wants. It is perplexing. I don't think he wants to take us with him to the new organization,' I said, wanting to change the conversation.

'Come on, let's leave. The traffic will get bad in a few minutes and we will be stuck on the highway!' I heard Payal's voice from behind.

'Okay, you leave now. I will call you later when you are in your room. Take care and ask Payal to drive carefully,' I said knowing that Rajni had to leave now. Then I wondered how annoying Payal could be at times. She had to have her way with everything. I just could not understand how Rajni managed with a beast like Payal.

'Bye! You drive carefully too. Will wait for your call!' said Rajni before I heard a click on the other end.

I locked my computer and walked over to Subbu's desk, unable to concentrate on the code. It was getting harder to work with so much action around.

~

'What are you doing?' I asked Subbu.

'Nothing, I was just checking for flight tickets home,' replied Subbu continuing his search.

'When are you going home? You never told us about the trip?' I asked.

'Dad called me this morning. There have been some problems with the house we bought a few years back. I need to go and help him sort out the issues. My parents are also trying to finalize a match for my younger sister,' he replied 'I think a week away from work would be good for me as well.'

Subbu was still glued to the web page that showed various options and the prices for tickets to Chennai when I walked over to Parag's desk, not wanting to disturb Subbu any longer.

'I just can't concentrate on the work. When do you think we should leave for Shiva's?' I asked, smiling at Parag.

'It is nearly 6 p.m. I think we should leave now and have a few drinks before AM joins us. It would brace us for whatever crap AM has in store for us.' Parag locked his computer and stood up. 'Let's leave, guys!' he shouted to the group before walking off in the direction of the restroom.

Bhau looked up at me innocently 'Are we leaving now?' We walked to the coffee machine to get something to drink. Thinking about Shiva's and AM was making me thirsty.

While we sipped water, Parag was back from the restroom. We walked towards the lift and waited for Subbu to join us.

Subbu shouted as he rushed past us, towards the printer, 'Give me a moment, guys!' He collected printouts of his tickets and joined us at the lift.

'So, when are you leaving?' I asked.

'Soon. It is none of your business,' Subbu replied curtly. He could be very obscure and hard to understand at times. He had the not-so-wonderful quality of making you feel unwanted, rather like a miscreant who had made the mistake of trespassing into his sanctuary. I tried my best to ignore Subbu's reaction, but it was hard. I swallowed my pride before following the others into the lift.

~

Bhau and I walked over to the corner table while Subbu and Parag headed to the neighbouring shop to fetch the drinks. They returned a short while later with four bottles of cider. I sipped my bottle and ignored the small talk around me. I was still annoyed with Subbu.

'Did I keep you guys waiting long?' I heard a voice from behind me. AM pulled a chair from the neighbouring table and sat down.

'Can I get you a drink?' volunteered Subbu.

'Yes, please, I will have the same thing you guys are having,' AM replied. He looked rather pale and seemed to have aged a lot since we had last seen him.

We waited uncomfortably for Subbu to return with AM's drink. AM was wearing a simple white shirt and black trousers. The shirt was peeping out from his pants. This was a different AM we were seeing. I had never seen him anything but impeccably dressed.

AM cleared his throat, breaking the silence, while we continued looking at him hoping that he would finish what he wanted to say and leave.

'How is work? I hope you are nearly done with the code that needs to be delivered on Friday,' he said smiling amicably at us.

None of us replied.

Was this why he had called us here? What an asshole! I thought, finding it hard to control myself.

AM smiled, hoping to release the tension. He seemed to have read my thoughts. 'I am sure you people have got the delivery under control. That is not what I wanted to speak to you about,' AM continued. 'My son is four years old. He is a smart little guy,' said AM ruefully. He seemed to suddenly have moved far away from us, lost in thoughts of his own.

I looked around at the others confused with why AM was letting us in on his family details.

Wasn't AM planning on leaving the organization? What was the point in telling us this crap?

'Ravi, my son, is suffering from cerebral palsy. I have been running around hospitals in Delhi trying to find a cure.' I could see tears well up inside AM's eyes as he said this. I was afraid AM was about to break down. It was hard to believe that this was the same AM whose supreme goal in life had been to torment us.

'I know you are all confused and wondering why I am telling you all this, but please be patient and let me finish. I probably should have spoken to you earlier, but I hope it is still not too late,' AM continued. None of our parents were doctors, and we personally did not know anyone who could help AM. I was getting restless. I fiddled with the empty bottle.

'Why don't you allow me to get you one more drink?' said AM, noticing my restlessness.

AM looked helplessly around the hotel for a waiter who would take his order, before turning towards us, completely lost.

'In here, you need to get your own drinks,' said Parag,

smiling as he stood up.

Subbu joined Parag as Parag started walking to the till.

'Hold on, the drinks are on me,' said AM extending a Rs 500 note to Parag.

AM waited for the drinks to arrive before continuing.

'Aman has been very helpful in locating a doctor in Bangalore who has agreed to help Ravi. The doctor wants us to travel to the US. I know there isn't much hope, but I just don't want to leave any stone unturned. We are leaving for the USA next month. I am trying to sort all the loose ends here before moving to the US.'

So AM wants us to help him move stuff and sort out things in Delhi, I thought.

'I know you are not in the least interested in my personal life, but it makes my task a lot easier after having told you all this. I don't want you people to sympathize with me, I am sure it is going to be hard doing that after you hear what I want to tell you,' AM paused and took one more sip from his bottle.

AM held the bottle to his mouth for a long time before continuing; he was finding it hard to talk.

'Aman is not a bad man. He is just a little too competitive and wants to grow fast in the organization.' He was looking at the wall on the far corner, away from us as he said this.

Was AM Aman's stooge who was trying to placate us after what had happened on Friday, I wondered? I hated AM even more now.

AM stopped speaking and looked away as he wiped the tears from his eyes.

None of us spoke for quite some time, we drank silently.

AM finished his bottle before suddenly walking out from the restaurant.

'What was that?' shouted Subbu. 'We already knew that Aman was God. He need not have sent a stooge to tell us that!' Subbu looked furious.

We looked around perplexed trying to make sense of AM's sudden reaction, while Subbu continued abusing him. It was a while before Parag spotted AM returning to our table.

'Hush! AM is coming back,' said Parag.

'Oh, let him! I don't care if he hears me,' retorted Subbu.

'I am sorry, guys; I just needed some fresh air. I am not going to keep you long I promise,' AM apologized. 'Let me just finish what I have to say very quickly,' he said, before taking his seat. 'I have been contemplating leaving this organization and moving to the US for a long time. I hope it is not too late now. I was frightened of the change and did not want to leave the comfortable position I had here. I was probably like all the others, unable to make the final decision. The last few months have been tough, but, looking back, I have little to complain about. I was finally able to make my decision and I wanted to apologize before I left. I hope knowing my side of the story will make it easier for you to forgive me.' AM looked around at us, probably hoping to find a glimmer of agreement or sympathy with what he was saying.

'It was four months back when I first noticed something wrong with the quality of people who had recently joined our team. I requested details from HR and found that most of them did not have good credentials. You know at our company we have always been very particular about the educational and employment credentials. We only recruit the best in the market.'

AM looked at our faces again before continuing.

'On making further inquiries, I learned that they were all recruited because of very strong referrals from Aman. I tried to find out the interview records and, to my surprise, most of the interviews were done by people like Anup.'

AM stopped to look at me before quickly adding, 'I am sorry, I don't have anything against you conducting interviews. All I wanted to convey was that Aman only used people who were technically weak or had little experience in conducting interviews. Aman probably used his power and forced you people into providing good feedback.'

I suddenly realized that I had been party to Aman's ploy. It all added up! Now I knew the answer to why Aman had not wanted Bhau conducting interviews for him.

AM waited for what he said to settle in before continuing, 'I confronted Aman about it and he initially refuted all my accusations, but, when I followed it up with proof from my findings, he warned me of dire consequences if I told anyone. Not wanting a confrontation after having seen Aman wield his powers and contacts at getting things sorted out in his favour earlier, I tried to ignore everything around me. It was initially very hard to do so, but, with problems at home, with my son and other developments it was easy to ignore everything that happened around me. The ghosts came back to haunt me last month when I was completing your appraisals. I had filled in all the review feedbacks and had wanted a consensus from Aman since he shared the responsibilities of managing the team with me. I invited Aman to a meeting, hoping to go through the reviews before finally forwarding them to the HR.

'Things were moving smoothly till we came to Chetan's form. Aman was surprised that I had filled in a request for

Chetan's promotion. He wanted me to change it. He pulled out your reviews next and was rather annoyed that I had given Subbu and Anup a good rating. Aman felt that you guys were not up to the mark and hence should not be getting a good feedback. Aman told me that he had lined up someone from outside the organization to take the position I wanted to promote Chetan to. Things started going out of control between us as I became adamant. We were down to shouting at each other. Anup had noticed the fight that evening when he came to collect coffee,' AM stopped to look at me.

'Yes,' I said, unsure of what was expected from me.

'Aman had a ferocious look on his face that night, and, for the first time, I was frightened enough to decide that I had to leave the organization. Aman had warned me, "I don't think things are working out between us, Arun. You are trying to force me into action. I don't want to hurt you. Do you know how many contacts I have in this organization?" What happened next is clear to all of you. I don't think you need help in deciphering that.' AM placed his head between his palms and let it stay there for a long time.

'Arun,' said Parag after the long silence.

'No, please, I don't want any of your sympathies. I feel much better now after having told you all this. All I wanted to ask from you is to please be careful of Aman. I wish you all the best for your future,' he blurted out before rushing outside the hotel.

AM was gone before we had time to react.

AM was gone forever, away from all the turmoil.

And AM probably had a peaceful sleep that night while Subbu, Parag, Bhau and I wrestled with fear and confusion.

20

THE LAST STONE

As the dice continues to roll, slowly but steadily the numbers are visible, but only time will tell whom they favour.

It was 9.00 p.m. when Dad and I reached home that night. We were having a quiet dinner when my phone started ringing. I rushed to pick the phone up, fearing it was Rajni. I did not want Mom answering Rajni's call.

It was Subbu.

'Hello,' I said into the phone.

'What are you doing?' asked Subbu.

'Eating,' I replied, still a little angry with Subbu.

'Okay. Do you know your way around Vasant Kunj? I am on my way to your house. Get ready quickly and I will pick you up!' Subbu disconnected before I had a chance to ask him any further questions.

'I have to leave, but will be back in a few minutes,' I said taking my seat at the dinner table.

Both Mom and Dad looked at me, surprised at the sudden development.

'Subbu is going to the hospital, and he wants me to accompany him,' I lied. 'One of Subbu's relatives is ill.' It had been so easy to lie! I thought.

I had built up a whole story within seconds. Dad volunteered to join Subbu and me, but I refused his offer as gently as I could. I pulled out a pair of jeans and a T-shirt and threw my night suit on the bed.

~

'Where are we going?' I asked Subbu as he pulled the bike over to our gate where I had been waiting for him.

'Just sit behind me and I will explain,' said Subbu handing me a piece of paper with an address scribbled on it.

'Whose house is this?' I asked completely lost by now.

'Tell me the directions. I will explain as we drive. It is already very late now, Priyanka will be asleep before we reach her place,' replied Subbu as he revved the bike towards Vasant Kunj.

It was hard to hear much over the noise, and I decided that there was no point in trying to have a logical conversation with Subbu.

I held tight to the seat, providing Subbu with the directions. As we passed the Spinal Injuries Centre, I could see a few lights at the hospital. We reached Priyanka's block around 10.30 p.m.

'Wait here,' said Subbu as he walked away from the bike towards what I thought was Priyanka's flat.

When Subbu did not return for a while, I started getting restless and contemplated leaving the bike and heading back home. I probably would have done just that had it not been so late in the night. Realizing that it would be hard finding transport, I forced myself to wait. Subbu returned fifteen minutes later. He seemed to be pleased with the way things had gone. He had a smile on his face as he mounted the bike and signalled me to take the seat behind him.

'Let's leave,' said Subbu before starting the bike.

Was Subbu having an affair with Priyanka? What the hell was he doing this late in the night with Priyanka? Could all this not have waited till tomorrow? Many other questions flooded my mind as we sped along the highway. Subbu seemed to be driving towards our office.

He parked the bike in front of Shiva's forty minutes later.

'Listen carefully,' said Subbu, glaring into my eyes. I was frightened by the look in his eyes unsure of what he intended to do but was too scared to question him. I gulped down my anxiety as Subbu continued speaking.

'I don't want you to talk about tonight with anyone. Not even Bhau or Parag have to know anything about tonight.' Subbu stressed on the last part of the sentence.

I was so frightened that I would have agreed to anything that Subbu had wanted from me.

I nodded my head as Subbu continued. 'I am sure you will not have to tell them much; they will soon learn about it . . .' This time he had a smile on his face. 'You sit here at Shiva's and wait till I get back. I need to fetch a few things from the office. Don't leave this place until I am back . . . understand?'

I felt a chill run though me. I bought a cigarette and lighted it unsteadily before taking a seat. Subbu had a few puffs from mine before walking off resolutely towards the office.

I sat on the chair at Shiva's, fighting my urge to follow him to the office. I began rationalizing my thoughts and trying to make a decision to sit or go in. I was feeling very sleepy, and the last thing I wanted to do was walk into office and look at my computer.

Was Subbu leaving the next day? He probably was, I thought. He probably wanted to meet his love Priyanka one more time before he went home to Chennai. Things started adding up now. Subbu had wanted me to join him since I knew the roads and would save him the trouble of locating Priyanka's house.

I felt very smart sitting on the chair and puffing the cigarette. Then I got up and bought myself a cup of tea from the corner stall before heading back to my seat. Shiva's was slowly closing down for the night. I looked at my watch; it was 11.30 p.m. Subbu had been gone for more than fifteen minutes.

I finished a second cigarette, yet there was still no sign of Subbu. It was getting cold. Shiva's was now desolate except for the lone bulb that still burned. The cigarette stall owner was pulling down the shutters. It was nearly forty-five minutes since Subbu had left. I walked across to the stall and bought a few more cigarettes, not having enough money for the pack. I had forgotten to collect my wallet in the hurry.

I hoped Subbu would be back soon as I paced around restlessly. I contemplated checking on him at the office. I even walked half the distance to the office, but retraced my steps when I recollected the look Subbu had on his face.

Subbu finally returned after a little more than an hour.

'Let's go,' Subbu said, unlocking the bike. Subbu had a satisfied look on his face and he seemed rather pleased with himself. He thought it unnecessary to provide me with any explanations. I again helped Subbu with directions to Priyanka's house. Subbu rushed over to her flat while I waited with the bike again. This time he was back quickly.

Subbu finally dropped me home around 1.30 a.m.

'Hope you people have lot of fun tomorrow. I am so sorry that I am going to miss it,' said Subbu before whizzing away.

I stood there at the gate watching Subbu's back, wondering what had happened that night. I walked home still unsteady from the events of the night. Thankfully, Mom had been too sleepy to ask me many questions.

I immediately went to bed and slept blissfully unaware that the dice had been rolled.

21

THE NEW DAWN

I was still very sleepy when I walked into office the next morning. Bhau and Parag were already in. They were both sitting in Bhau's cubicle engrossed in something on his computer screen.

Subbu was still to get in. I greeted Bhau and Parag before heading to my seat. They were so engrossed that they failed to notice me.

I logged on and waited for the computer to start.

The phone on my desk started buzzing.

Who could be calling me this early in the morning, I wondered?

'Hello!' I said, recognizing the voice on the other end. It was Rajni. She sounded very excited. 'Did you check your mail?' she asked, shouting into the phone to make her voice heard over the din behind her.

'No, I just got in,' I replied, not understanding what the ruckus was about. All this was only adding to the confusion from last night.

'Is Subbu in yet?' she shouted. Why the hell was Rajni so excited about Subbu suddenly?

The computer had logged me on and was awaiting further instructions. I clicked on the Outlook icon.

'No, Subbu is not in. Why? Is something wrong?' I asked, wanting to know more details.

There obviously was something that I had completely missed.

'Did you check your emails?' shouted Parag before sinking back into whatever he was doing with Bhau. There were very few emails in my inbox. I scrolled down trying to find the email that was causing all the fuss.

I could not find any email other than a few from my friends who surely would not have emailed Rajni and Parag.

'I don't see any email,' I shouted back.

'How about the email from Subbu? Don't you have the email from Subbu in your inbox?' Rajni sounded annoyed at my inability to find the email.

I clicked on Subbu's email.

'The last stone' read the subject on the email.

Hi All,

I am sure you are surprised to find this email in your inbox early in the morning, but, don't worry, there is enough in this email to probably make you not want to work for the rest of your lives!

Mr Aman Sharma, a legend with whom I had the privilege of working with, is a man of many talents. I hope this email is good enough to provide him with all the credit he rightly deserves.

Find attached the scanned copies of interview recommendations and feedbacks provided by Aman Sharma. I am attaching just a few so that your mailboxes don't clog. I am not even sure if the mail would make it through the network if I did attach all of them.

In addition to these, also find a copy of the great man's CV. I don't even know if the company he worked before joining us even exists.

The above is just half the story because the other half lies in the bills and claims that Mr Aman has submitted to the company.

I am sure there will be many other questions you might have once you see the bills.

I have attached a few big bills, but, if you are interested in details, then you could find spare copies that I have placed at various locations in the office.

I guess I will have to leave now as this should be more than enough.

Aman: I will look for you if I ever want to destroy a country or bring down a government.

—Subbu the Seeker.

Dial 007 for Super Detective Subbu the Man.

22

THE FINAL CHAPTER

We never saw Aman again.

Someone had informed him about the happenings at office and he never showed up at work that day.

All the people who had been recruited by Aman were re-interviewed, many of them were sacked.

KK had visited our cubicles quite a few times that day in order to enquire if we knew anything about Subbu's whereabouts.

It took nearly a month before the dust settled down and except for a few, most of the things had returned to as they had been before.

KK had advised me to start looking for a new job. The company was not going to sack me, but, since I was involved in the interviews with Aman, it was in my best interests that I left the organization.

I had put in my papers and was still deciding what I needed to do next. I had always wanted to be a writer and this was a good opportunity to start working on it. Rajni and I spent a lot of time together during my last few days at the office.

Rajni had been very supportive throughout. She is, to date, probably my only fan who loves to read what I write. She encourages me with her positive comments and eggs me on to taking writing seriously. She is very positive that one day I will make it as a great writer, and she would then no longer need to work, but until then, one of us has to work.

Our parents had been against Rajni and me marrying. My Dad could never come to terms with the fact that I was asked to leave the organization. Mom had also been shattered but she could do little to help me. I had no option but to leave the house.

Rajni too walked out on her family. We have rented a small flat near the office so that it is easy for Rajni to go to work.

~

I still remember the blue shirt I had bought for Rajni's birthday from Shoppers Stop. Rajni had worn the same shirt when she left her home for the last time to join me at the registrar's office. I wonder if things would have turned out differently had I found the red shirt that day.

~

Rajni and I are used to a daily routine now: I wake up in the morning to cook breakfast for us while she gets dressed for work. I sometimes even walk her to the office. When I am not in a mood for writing, I cook lunch and Rajni comes home during lunchtime. I also cook dinner on the days when I am able do little writing.

On weekends, we usually go out to the malls, or Rajni

busies herself with the cooking. She still finds it hard to digest the fact that I do all the household tasks and insists that I should not enter the kitchen when she is home. I thank my lucky stars for having found Rajni and friends like Parag, Bhau, and Subbu.

We are still in touch with Parag and Bhau. Parag calls me at least once a week. We travel to Lucknow every now and then to meet Parag and Nidhi. They had a beautiful daughter last month. Rajni and I went down to Lucknow for a week to be with them.

Parag resigned a few months after I left the company. He and Nidhi moved to Lucknow where they now teach at a college. Bhau has moved to Pune with a research company. He has a team of twenty people who are working on a new software. He tells me that the new software is soon going to revolutionize the software market forever. I am sure it will. For all the hard work Bhau puts in, the software has to turn out great.

We were never able to locate Subbu.

His phone had been switched off ever since the morning that we last saw him. None us knew where Subbu lived. After all, the address Subbu had provided to the company had been fake. He will always remain a mystery for us.

~

It is time for me to start cooking. Rajni should be home in an hour. I want to cook her something nice to celebrate the completion of this novel. It is our second anniversary tomorrow. I hope Rajni is able to convince her manager to give her a day off from work.

Oh! There is just one more thing, I wanted to add. Rajni and I are flying to Dublin next month on a company assignment. Rajni had long been asked to go to Dublin for the project but we had been putting it off till I could complete the book.

Rajni is very excited about the trip.

I will have to stop now, as there is a lot of work to do!

EPILOGUE

Subbu's Story

Let me take the story forward. That night, after hearing what AM had to say and having looked at the faces of Parag, Bhau and Anup, my heart pained like it had done only once before. I decided that I had to sort things out for my friends.

I knew what needed to be done. I borrowed Bhau's bike and after dropping him at his residence, I called Priyanka up and asked her for a big favour. I had known that she would refuse to cooperate if she learnt the real reason because she would be running a big risk by helping me, if I was caught. So I asked Priyanka for the keys to the filing cabinets where all employee records and other details were placed. I told her that I wanted to clear a few fake bills that I had submitted by mistake the month before. I added that I wanted to play it safe since I was planning to leave the organization and did not want to risk being caught when they verified all my past details as a part of the releasing process.

Fortunately, Priyanka was dumb enough to believe me. And she had expenses to take care of; she always spends more than what she earns. So when I offered money, she agreed on a sum of Rs 5000 after a lot of haggling. I

242

would have happily paid more, but I did not want her to doubt my true intentions.

Then I called Anup, because I did not know the routes around Delhi, and the last thing I wanted that night was to get lost.

When we reached Priyanka's house I made Anup wait near the bike. I collected the keys from Priyanka, paid her the money and promised to return that night to hand the keys back. We agreed that I would place the keys under the flower pot outside her flat as it would be too late in the night by the time I got back.

~

I walked into office after entering my name in the register. Then I swiped my card and headed straight for the HR cubicles. What happened next was simple. I quickly found the files. I scanned the details and also photocopied them just in case my email did not make it through. I placed the files at various locations inside the office and finally sent the email before walking out.

We drove back to Priyanka's house and dropped the keys. The next morning I handed the bike to Parag as he lived just a stone's throw from my flat. I already had the tickets booked so all I needed to do was pack my bags and head to the airport. I had remembered to collect my personal files on the way out from office. I wanted to make sure that none of my personal details remained with the organization.

Ah! Just before I finish, you must still be wondering why Parag had thanked me that evening. I had asked Nidhi out for a coffee on Monday evening. Nidhi had reluctantly agreed to my offer mistaking my intentions. At the coffee shop I shared with Nidhi the true story about Syalini and me. She was the first and probably the only person who knows all the details about what had gone on in my mind the day I had left Chennai for Delhi. She had tears in her eyes as she heard about our fates.

'Nidhi it is very simple to sacrifice your happiness and become a martyr,' I had said. 'You seem to have done the easiest thing by running away from the problem. You think Pooja is going to be happy because of your sacrifice?' I had laughed out loud as I had said that.

I had learnt that laughing helped me forget my pain and take my mind away from my past. 'I have been running away from my life since the day I left Chennai,' I said once I regained control. 'Nidhi, you would be doing the most foolish and wrong thing of your life if you stood by your decision. You would be lying to yourself if you are convinced that Parag and you could live a normal life after this. And besides, why would you want to curse Pooja into a future with a person who can never be hers from his heart? Would it not be better to kill Pooja instead of blessing her with a life of misery and pain?

'Pooja does not know Parag beyond the few hours they usually spent talking on phone. They have met each other only twice, that too for a few hours. I know Pooja does not deserve this but the pain she feels when she learns about Parag and you would leave her after a few months. On the other hand the pain you will bestow on her by forcing Parag into marrying her will stay with her for life. And probably gnaw at her for the rest of her life. Please think before you take any further steps.' Then I dropped Nidhi to her house before heading to Shiva's for a few drinks.

I sat at Shiva's relishing the last few days in Delhi. I had sensed that I was soon going back home to Chennai . . . to my family and memories of Syalini . . .

ACKNOWLEDGEMENTS

I started my career in late 1999, a time when the Indian IT industry suffered its first tremors. The period signalled the end of unrestrained growth.

I was new and still carried the illusion of infallibility that everyone who enters this industry harbours. But the illusion soon shattered. During those weeks I and my colleagues dreaded every moment, especially, after the clock struck four. We huddled in groups around the lone phone that adored our cubicle—those were the days when we had four people to one big cubicle, sharing a phone; it was long before the Google revolution, a time when Hotmail still ruled the roost—for every time the phone rang after 4 p.m. it confirmed our worst fears that one of us was about to leave the company. Every exit was shrouded in mystery and every person leaving had a story to tell. Though the recovery was fast and most of my friends who were laid-off soon had a job, eight years later when I started this book, those weeks of 2000 were still strongly etched on my mind.

The skeleton on which the book was later developed was written in early 2008. I had continued to add pages, egged on by Chhaya and Prabhat who were ever so enthusiastic to read the next instalment. I emailed the story to my friend Joe Culley who has been a constant encouragement. Joe forwarded the script to his friend Kathy who was kind enough to look at the book and provide her valuable inputs.

Meanwhile I emailed the book to my friends Binu, Amita, Amit, Vidhya and Mani.

Binu, Vidhya, Amita and Samiksha (Amit's wife) got back with positive comments. The fact that all of them had been able to complete the book in a single sitting provided me with the confidence.

I had made my decision by mid 2008. And with KT's help I was able to make copies of the book and mail it to the publishers. And the rest as they say is history.

I thank all my friends for having helped me with their encouraging words when I needed them the most. A special thanks to my dad for having read the entire book—for this is the only novel that he has ever finished reading. I would also like to thank Vaishali and Paloma for their valuable inputs, for helping me to bring the book to its current shape and to Penguin for providing me a platform. Last but not the least, thank you Deepthi for giving me a patient hearing through all my ramblings about the book, and also helping me with this acknowledgement.